A Comedy in Four Chapters

by
DEL SHORES

Song "SORDID LIVES"
by
Margot Rose & Beverly Nero

A SAMUEL FRENCH ACTING EDITION

SAMUEL FRENCH

FOUNDED 1830

New York Hollywood London Toronto

SAMUELFRENCH.COM

ISBN   978-0-573-63043-9   Printed in U.S.A.   #21435

IMPORTANT BILLING AND CREDIT REQUIREMENTS

All producers of *SORDID LIVES* *must* give credit to the Author of the Play in all programs distributed in connection with performances of the Play and in all instances in which the title of the Play appears for purposes of advertising, publicizing or otherwise exploiting the Play and/or a production. The name of the Author *must* appear on a separate line on which no other name appears, immediately following the title, and *must* appear in size of type not less than fifty percent the size of the title type.

This edition includes a new appendix where Del Shores has added the character "Juanita" from the film version.

SORDID LIVES was originally produced by Del Shores in association with Jeff Murray and Nicolette Chaffey for Theatre/Theater in Hollywood, California, May 11, 1996. It was directed by Del Shores; the set was by Newell Alexander; the lights were by Evan Bartoletti; the sound was by Scott Watson; hair, wigs and make-up design were by Simón Schwarz; and costumes were by Jim Eckerd. Associate producers were John Hagen and Philece Sampler; the production stage manager was John Hagen; the assistant stage managers were Diana Garrett, Chris Garrett, Tyler Hansen and Steve Thomas. The song "Sordid Lives" was written by Margot Rose and Beverly Nero. The cast in order of appearance, was as follows:

BITSY MAE HARLING	Margot Rose
TY WILLIAMSON	Kirk Geiger
SISSY HICKEY	Beth Grant
NOLETA NETHERCOTT	Patrika Darbo
LATRELLE WILLIAMSON	Mary-Margaret Lewis
LAVONDA DUPREE	Ann Walker
G.W. NETHERCOTT	Mitch Carter
WARDELL "BUBBA" OWENS	Newell Alexander
ODELL OWENS	Earl Bullock
DR. EVE BOLINGER	Rosemary Alexander
EARL "BROTHER BOY" INGRAM	Leslie Jordan
REV. BARNES	Earl Bullock

Also appearing in the year-long run were:

Jane George, Beverly Nero, Judy Quay (Bitsy); Robert Lewis Stephenson (Ty); Brenda Hillhouse, Ann Walker, Sharon Madden, Sandra Lafferty (Sissy); Loma Scott, Beth Grant (Noleta); Rosemary Alexander (Latrelle); Philece Sampler, Dale Dickey (LaVonda); Terry Brannon, Del Shores (Wardell); Philece Sampler (Dr. Eve); Del Shores, Tyler Hansen, Charlie Dell (Brother Boy).

All hymns public domain. ("Uncloudy Day", "Coming Home", "In The Sweet By and By" and "Just As I Am")

THE CAST

BITSY MAE HARLING—the guitar playing ex-con singer.

TY WILLIAMSON—27, a beautiful gay man on a journey.

SISSY HICKEY—mid 50's, the caretaker who picked the wrong day to quit smoking.

NOLETA NETHERCOTT—early 40's the angry overweight betrayed housewife.

LATRELLE WILLIAMSON—early 50's, Ty's uptight, proper mother.

LA VONDA DUPREE—late 40's, Latrelle's liberal-minded worldly sister.

G.W. NETERCOTT—late 40's, the distraught legless Vietnam Vet.

WARDELL "BUBBA" OWENS—late 40's, the former gay-bashing remorseful bartender.

ODELL OWENS—mid 40's, Wardell's worthless story-telling brother.

DR. EVE BOLINGER—late 40's, the over-sexed pill-popping, alchoholic therapist.

EARL "BROTHER BOY" INGRAM—late 40's, the Tammy Wynette obsessed transvestite.

REV. BARNES—the Southern Baptist preacher. (Author's suggestion is to double cast with the actor who plays ODELL.)

THE SETTINGS

THE TIME
July 24th & 25th, 1998

AUTHOR'S NOTE: These people are real. Don't play them as cartoons, please. Each chapter may be pulled out and produced as a One Act (but you still have to pay royalties!).

FOR

Newell & Rosemary
Rebecca & Caroline

For their unconditional love and acceptance

CHAPTER ONE

Nicotine Fit

(In the darkness, we hear a guitar strum. A spot hits BITSY MAE HARLING, who is standing downstage left in front of a mike. She gives the audience a look, then sings.)

BITSY. *(Slow country rhythm.)*
"Who's to judge who's a saint and who's a sinner?
Lord it's tough enuf to trudge from brunch to dinner.
We seek the light of truth between our white lies.
And sleep away our youth under tattle-tale skies.

(Picks up tempo.)

Who's to say who's a sinner and who's a saint?
Who's to say who you can love and who you cain't?
It's easy for the pot to call the kettle black
When jealous of the hot'n lusty sordid lives they lack.

Ain't it a bitch sortin' out our sordid lives?
It's a bitch when you come to realize,
Crack yerself a box of Cracker Jack
You could get a really shitty prize!

7

It's a bitch sortin' out our sordid lives!

We struggle comin' down the shoot to take our first breath.
Then we struggle for acceptance from birth to death.
But the Lord's too busy tryin' to keep the world on it's feet.
He ain't got time to give a shit 'bout what goes on between
    the sheets.

Ain't it a bitch sortin' out our sordid lives?
It's a bitch when you come to realize,
Crack yerself a box of Cracker Jack
You could get a really shitty prize!
It's a bitch sortin' out our sorry little sordid lives!"

(Blackout.)

(In the darkness, BITSY moves the mike and exits.
Dim lights come up only on TY, late 20's, movie star good looks,
*   sitting on a chair downstage center. He talks to his therapist*
*   [the audience].)*

TY. You're my twenty-seventh therapist in three years.
(Searching.) Where to start...? I'm from the South. Texas actually.
I was raised rigid Southern Baptist. I'm an actor. And I'm gay.
Now you know why I've needed twenty-seven therapists in the
past three years. *(Pause.)* I always hate... okay... let's see. Oh! I had
a dream last night. I know you guys love dreams. It was about Ruth
Buzzi. From "Laugh-In." When I was a little boy, I was never
allowed to watch "Laugh-In." "Too vulgar and risqué" my Mama
used to say. But one summer, I spent three weeks with my Aunt
LaVonda and she let me watch it three Mondays in a row. I felt so

sneaky and evil. I liked that feeling. *(Thinks.)* I still do. Aunt
LaVonda was so cool she swore me to secrecy. "What ya Mama
don't know won't hurt her, but if ya Mama did know, she hurt us
both!" I love that woman. She used to cuss in front of me. In fact,
the first time I heard the word "fuck", it came out of her mouth.
She's great. Now I watch it all the time. On cable..."Laugh In"...
re-runs. It did not date well. So anyway, Ruth Buzzi was playing
that old prude on the park bench, you know, in my dream. And
Artie Johnson was there. And she got all offended and started hitting him on the head with her purse. Then, it went all weird. Ruth's
wig fell off and she was a man. Then she stopped beating on Artie
and they looked at each other. Longingly. Then they started kissing
and ripping at each other's clothes. And Ruth had falsies on and
Artie just tore 'em off. And she was this man! With a beautiful
body—incredible pecs and a ripped stomach...great ass. Kinda
looked like Antonio Sabato, Jr.—with Ruth Buzzi's face. And the
most beautiful cock you have ever seen. Ruth was hung like a
horse. Artie looked awful though. He was all flabby and pasty, and
he had this little bitty thumb dick. But you know, Ruth didn't seem
to mind. They just started going at it on that park bench a mile a
minute. I woke up with a hard on, totally turned on by Ruth Buzzi's
old prude woman as a man. *(Pause.)* What do you think that
means?

(Lights fade to black.)

SISSY. *(In blackout.)* Well, I tell you one thang. I sure as hell
woundn'ta quit smoking if I'da known Sister was gonna die.

*(Full lights come up and we are in the tackily decorated living
room/dining area of SISSY HICKEY'S house. TY's chair has*

moved and is now part of the decor which includes a couch, downstage, "TY's" chair next to it, left of the couch. Center stage, left, a telephone table sits. A dining room table is further upstage, right. SISSY, mid 50's, is talking on the phone while cleaning up. She has one of those long telephone cords that she expertly tosses and pulls around as she scurries about. The dining table is full of covered dishes, all shapes and sizes.)

SISSY. Three days now and I'm just about to die myself. Hold on. *(She pulls on a rubber band that she's wearing on her arm and pops herself with it.)* Ouch! *(Listens.)* Oh nothing. *(Pause.)* Well, if you must know, it's a little quit smokin' therapy that Roger over at the Beehive shared with me while he was backcombing my hair. He paid two thousand dollars at this clinic over in Snyder and they give him a rubber band. Told him to pop his arm with it ever' time he wanted a cigarette. Sat there for a week with a buncha other smokers, just talkin' about any ol' thang and watchin' the television while poppin' their arms. It's called Behavior Modifi... somethin' or 'nother. Roger can tell you the exact wordage. Anyway, it ain't workin'! *(Listens.)* Chorus girl kicks, huh?! This month's issue? Well, I've got it here somewhere. *(There is a knock at the door.)* Vera, I gotta go. Somebody else is at the door. *(Looks out window.)* Oh, Lord, it's Noleta Nethercott. I'll call you back. *(She hangs up and goes to the door.)* Woohoo.

NOLETA. *(O.S.)* Woohoo.

SISSY. Woohoo. *(Opens door.)* Hello, Noleta. Come on in.

(NOLETA NETHERCOTT, pretty, overweight and distraught, hands SISSY a tuna casserole as she enters.)

NOLETA. *(On the verge of tears.)* Hello, Sissy. I brung this. It's my mama's tuna casserole. You know, the one I always make with the Lays Potato Chips and the cream of mushroom soup.

SISSY. Well, thank you, Noleta. That was mighty nice of you given the circumstances and all. Are you all right?

NOLETA. I'm fine.

(NOLETA then bursts into tears.)

SISSY. Oh hon!

(SISSY hugs NOLETA.)

NOLETA. *(Between sobs.)* I just can't believe it. Ever'body's laughing at me, Sissy. G.W. has made a complete fool outta me. Can I bum a cigarette, please?

SISSY. Oh, Lord, hon. I quit. Three days ago. Threw `em all away. Why don't you set down and I'll get you a nice glass of ice tea. Would you like a Valium?

NOLETA. Uh-huh.

(SISSY exits for the tea as NOLETA moves to the food table and begins fixing herself a plate.)

NOLETA. I mean, this has to be awkward for you, Sissy. My husband killed your sister with his, um... *(Crying.)* I threw him out. I threw his sorry ass out, Sissy. Threw all his stuff out on the front lawn. If he don't git it by tonight, I'm gonna have a yard sale! But what am I gonna do now?

SISSY. Aw, hon.

(SISSY hands her the tea and moves to the telephone table to find the Valium in her purse.)

NOLETA. I mean, I have no skills. I'm just a mama and a wife. What the hell am I suppose to do now!?
SISSY. Awwwww.

(NOLETA continues to wail as SISSY finds the pills and pulls off a couple of Kleenex.)

SISSY. *(For NOLETA's benefit.)* Awwwww. *(Mutters.)* Shit.

(SISSY hands NOLETA the pills and Kleenex and sits.)

NOLETA. Thank you. I'm sorry. I shouldn't be telling you this seein's that your Sister died on account of my husband's...should I take one or two of these?
SISSY. I'd take two if I was you.
NOLETA. Okay.

(NOLETA downs the pills.)

SISSY. You'll feel a lot better when those kick in. *(Leans in.)* And you can tell me anythang you want, Noleta. I feel for you. I do. This whole thang is just one big... *(SISSY takes a Valium herself and chases it with tea.)*... unfortunate mess. Now don't get me wrong, I loved my sister dearly, but you and me are friends bottom line, and I'm here for you right now. You hear me talkin' to you? I mean it.
NOLETA. Thank you, Sissy. Where's LaVonda? I'm just so scared this is gonna affect our friendship. You know how close we are.

SISSY. I know. LaVonda and Latrelle went over to the funeral home to make all the arrangements. Latrelle is just beside herself. She is so high-strung. But don't you worry. You know LaVonda. She loves you like a sister. That ain't gonna change one iota. I'm gonna get you a re-fill.

(She takes NOLETA's plate and moves to the food table, filling it.)

NOLETA. Thank you. Today I was at the Shamrock, fillin' up. I just needed one more full tank for a complete set of them Dallas Cowboy mugs. And you know that trashy thang, Lynnette Walters, was talkin' to her friend that Gloria, other piece of trash, old man Holmes' youngest girl, the one with them two illegitimate mulatto kids. And they was staring at me, pointin', talkin' all hush-hush. Those two. All skinny in their tube-tops and short-shorts. Like I was some kind of circus freak or somethin'. Those two, Sissy. Of all people. Like they was better than me.

SISSY. Well, they're not.

NOLETA. I just went over to her window, threw down a twenty, didn't wait for my change or my Dallas Cowboy mug and left.

SISSY. Good.

NOLETA. Drove down Highway 84, sobbin'to high heaven, goin' nowhere. I finally had to pull over 'cause I couldn't see the road no more.

SISSY. Oh, hon.

NOLETA. I'm sorry. I shouldn't be troublin' you. You've got enough on your mind.

(NOLETA gets up and takes some chicken and a couple of biscuits from her plate, wrapping them in her napkin.)

NOLETA. I gotta go, Sissy. The kids get outta school at three and I gotta explain about G. W. I'm so sorry about Peggy. She was a good woman, in spite of— *(She starts crying again.)* Tell LaVonda to call me.

SISSY. I will. Those Valium oughta kick in any minute.

(SISSY runs and gets the bottle of pills and hands them to NOLETA.)

SISSY. Here! Take these with ya. I've got another bottle.
NOLETA. Thank you.

(NOLETA exits.)

SISSY. *(Calling after her.)* Bye, bye, hon. Thanks for the casserole. And you hold your head up, high, hear?!
NOLETA. *(O.S. between sobs.)* I'll try.
SISSY. *(False sincerity.)* I mean it. *(Closes door.)* Shit.

(She pops her arm. The phone rings. She runs for it and answers it.)

SISSY. Hello. Oh, hello Vera. No, I hadn't read it yet. Noleta just left. Well, we had a little talk. She's real upset. Who could blame her? *(Listens.)* I know it. I know it. I know it. I give her some Valium. Bless 'er heart. So Cosmo says that chorus girl kicks will distract you from a nicotine fit and it'll go away? Well, I don't know. I just don't thank I could do 'em worth a flyin' flit, and if I did, I cringe just to thank about somebody walkin' in on me and thinkin' I'm crazy. *(Listens, very serious.)* Huh-uh. Oh no. I don't think Brother Boy's mentally stable enough to come to the funeral. Last time I visited him, he thought he was Tammy Wynette. Had on a real pretty wig and a sequined pantsuit, though. And if you'd squint your eyes and kept a good distance away, he looked just like Tammy. In the early years. *(Listens.)* I know it, I know it. I know it. Tammy's gone now. Clotted lung or somethin'. She's sangin' with the angels now and they're lucky to have her. Bless 'er heart. Had more troubles than Christ on the cross. Honey when it came to life threatenin' illnesses, ol' Tammy was sorta the Elizabeth Taylor of country music.

(We hear a car drive up. SISSY runs for the door and looks out its window.)

SISSY. *(cont.)* I gotta git! That's Latrelle. Oooh. She does not look happy! Her and LaVonda've been at it all morning long. They never could git along and I refuse to referee any more. *(Listens.)* Well, thank you, hon. I need those prayers. Prayers mean so much. I'll see ya at the funeral. Bye bye. *(She hangs up, pops herself with the rubberband.)* Ouch!

(LATRELLE WILLIAMSON, early 50's, very proper, SISSY's niece, but only three years younger, bursts in the door.)

LATRELLE. *(Pissed.)* Well, you're just never gonna believe what she's done now! You just won't!
SISSY. *(Overlap.)* Well, what did—?
LATRELLE. *(Plowing on.)* LaVonda wants to bury Mama in that ugly ol' mink stole with the head still on it!
SISSY. *(Overlap.)* Well—
LATRELLE. I know that Mama loved that stole, but good Lord, Sissy, it's a hundred and eight degrees out and no person living or dead should be caught wearin' a mink stole in the middle of summer. It's not appropriate, it's not right and I will not have it! And I hope you will support me on this!

SISSY. Well I—

LATRELLE. I will not have her making a mockery of my Mama at her one and only funeral! It's just not gonna happen! Lord it's hot! Your air conditioner working?

SISSY. Yeah, but when it gets like this, it don't seem to help a lick.

LATRELLE. Probably needs Freon.

SISSY. *(Goes and fiddles with the thermostat.)* I never did like Sister's mink stole no ways. Gave me the heebbie-geebies with them glass eyes staring out at ya. 'Course she was awful partial to it.

LATRELLE. I know it. But it's summer, Sissy! Hot, hot summer! *(Rushes over and hugs Sissy.)* Oh, thank you, thank you! I knew you'd back me on this, I did.

SISSY. Well—

LATRELLE. But you know how she is. But she won't listen to me. I gotta go tittle.

SISSY. I—

LATRELLE. *(Rushes out of the room; O.S.)* Thank you.

SISSY. *(Stares after her.)* Shit! Damn! Shit! *(Then pops the rubberband.)* Ouch!

LATRELLE. *(O.S.)* Did you say somethin'?

SISSY. *(Calling.)* No. You want some ice tea? I just made a fresh batch!

LATRELLE. *(O.S.)* That'd be heaven. I'm parched.

(SISSY stares at the two glasses of tea on the coffee table, considers, then refills NOLETA's from her own. Then she walks over to the dining table.)

SISSY. There's enough food in here to feed Cox's army. Folks been droppin' by all mornin'.

*(LATRELLE re-enters adjusting her pantyhose. SISSY hands her
NOLETA's tea, then exits with NOLETA's dirty plate.)*

LATRELLE. Did anyone say anything?

SISSY. *(O.S.)* About what?

LATRELLE. You know, about the circumstances...*(Whispers.)*...surrounding Mama's death.

SISSY. *(Re-enters.)* Oh, that. Well, Noleta Nethercott was over
here. She brought by a tuna casserole. Her Mama's recipe. *(re:
casserole.)* That oughta be refrigerated. We will all get ptomaine.

*(SISSY exits with the casserole. LATRELLE pulls up her skirt and
starts adjusting her slip.)*

SISSY. *(O.S.)* It's all over town, Latrelle. I'm sorry.

(SISSY re-enters.)

LATRELLE. *(Whimpers.)* Oh. Well, I refuse to believe a word
of it. Someone started that vicious rumor. That's why I moved
away from this town. Mama was a good Christian woman and
ever'body knows that. *(Turns around.)* Is ever'thang straight back
there?

SISSY. Looks all right to me. Well, Latrelle, you know I'd
never say anything bad about my sister. I mean, she was like a second Mama to me bein's how much older she was. But honey, she
sorta just went a little crazy towards the end after'n your Daddy
died. Just kinda cut loose. Started honky tonkin' out at Bubba's
almost ever' night. Her best friend towards the end was Bitsy Mae
Harling.

LATRELLE. Bitsy Mae Harling who used to date blacks in
high school?

SISSY. The one in the same. She's been singing on the weekends out at Bubba's since she got out of jail. Said she was framed.

LATRELLE. Prison trash.

(SISSY laughs, which turns into a cough.)

LATRELLE. That's a cigarette cough.

SISSY. No shit.

LATRELLE. You're gonna die of lung cancer just like Aunt Berthie did. You mark my word. Lord, that was an awful death. She suffered so.

SISSY. Well, for your information, Miss Smarty Britches, I quit smokin'. Three days ago!

LATRELLE. Uh-huh. We'll see how long that lasts. Besides, the damage you have done to your lungs is most likely irreparable. I read all about it in a magazine at the doctor's office. *(Thinks.)* Bitsy Mae Harling and Mama.

SISSY. Yes' ma'am. Then a couple months ago, Sister started carryin' on with G.W. Nethercott and that was the beginnin' to—

LATRELLE. Stop! Just stop it! I don't want to talk about this anymore! *(Moves to the food table.)* I want to remember Mama the way I want to remember her and not shacked up in a motel room with a low-life with two wooden legs. Oooh, apple pie. You want a piece?

(LATRELLE sits and begins eating her pie.)

SISSY. No thanks. Maybe a little later. How's Ty? He still up in New York?

LATRELLE. *(Sighs long and hard, softly.)* Yes. Too busy to come to his one and only grandmother's funeral. Hon, this pie is good. Who made this?

SISSY. Evelyn Crawley. I guess I will have a little piece after all. I swear, I'm gonna get as big as Vera Lisso without my nicotine.

(SISSY moves to the table, cuts herself some pie and sits across from LATRELLE.)

LATRELLE. Oh my Lord! I saw Vera today. I stopped in at the Piggly Wiggly to get a cold drink and I had a craving for something sweet. My Lord, she has gotten big!

SISSY. You could move in.

LATRELLE. Well, I almost didn't recognize her.

SISSY. She can't even stand up behind that register no more. They got her a bar stool to sit on, and Leticia Bustamante...that sweet little Mexkin girl who works the other register...told me that Tom Ed had to reinforce that stool with lug nuts!

LATRELLE. I'll swear.

SISSY. Vera is so sweet, though. She always slips me a few extra Green Stamps and doesn't even bother to look at the expiration date on my coupons. She's my best friend.

LATRELLE. But why on God's green earth would anyone let themselves get that big?

SISSY. She says it's glandular.

LATRELLE. Glandular?

(They laugh.)

SISSY. Oh, I saw Ty in that Alpo commercial where the dog licks his face. That was real cute. Lord, he is so good lookin'. Y'all must be proud.

LATRELLE. Well, we're not. I mean, I like that commercial and all, but after he got off the soap opera, he started doin' theater, Sissy! Awful, awful stuff. He calls it art...I call it trash! Did this one play and begged me and Wilson to come up to New York and see him in it. Well, I was just dying to see Glenn Close in "Sunset Blvd.", so I talked Wilson into going up there. The play was called, oh I forget the name, some musical term..."Allegro"..."Alegre"—

SISSY. Crescendo?

LATRELLE. No. Whatever it was it had nothin' whatsoever to do with the subject matter. Anyhow, the play was going all nice like—and all of a sudden my son walks out on stage—naked! Buck naked, Sissy!!

SISSY. Sweet Jesus! Neked!

LATRELLE. And you could see everythang.

SISSY. His tallywhacker?

LATRELLE. Everything! And he was playing a...*(Whispers.)* ...homosexual—again! I just looked down at my lap until it was over. I have never been so humiliated in all my life. And you know what he had the audacity to do? Came up to us after and said, "So what'd ya think?" What'd I think?! What was I supposed to think!? Well, I just stared at him with my mouth open and he said, "Okay, let's go get some dinner." Wilson said we weren't ever going back to New York. Said it was worse than Los Angeles. I raised him better than that, Sissy. I did. Oh! And on top of everything, when we went to see "Sunset Blvd." the next night, Glenn Close had lost her voice and this other girl that I never had heard of in my life did the role of Norma Desmond...who they said had once had a part on "Rhoda", but I certainly didn't remember her. The entire trip was one big bust!

SISSY. *(Pause, not really listening.)* Well, that's too bad. I thought in that TV movie where he played that AIDS patient that he was real good. They had him lookin' like death warmed over. I wish they had given him a bigger part, though. Vera went to the bathroom and missed him altogether.

LATRELLE. But Sissy, these roles! There's a reoccurring theme here in case you haven't noticed. Except for the Alpo commercial. After that movie aired, I called him and told him, if you're gonna play a homosexual, why waste it on a bit part? Win an Academy Award for heaven's sake like that famous actor in that Spider Woman movie...or Tom Hanks in that other thing that I didn't particularly care for...but don't waste it on a bit part!

(A car drives up out front and LATRELLE runs over and looks out the door.)

LATRELLE. That's LaVonda! I can't believe the way she dresses. In public! Now you are gonna back me on this mink stole thing, aren't you?
SISSY. Well, um...
LATRELLE. *(re: LAVONDA.)* Struttin' like banty rooster.

(LATRELLE moves away from the door as LA VONDA DUPREE, LATRELLE's baby sister, the worldly one, late 40's, sashays in, wearing a bright yellow peasant blouse, off the shoulders, tight jeans, smoking a cigarette.)

LATRELLE. Well?!
LA VONDA. Well, what, Latrelle? Oh hello, Sissy, how're you, shug?

(They hug.)

SISSY. I'm fine.

(SISSY stares at LAVONDA's cigarette.)

LA VONDA. Look at all this food.

(She goes over and starts exploring and picking.)

LATRELLE. Where's the stole, LaVonda?

LA VONDA. On Mama, where it belongs!

LATRELLE. You're just doin' this out of spite, LaVonda Jean! Mama's gonna look like a fool wearin' a mink stole in this heat. We'll be the laughing stock in town.

LA VONDA. Unfortunately, we already are.

SISSY. Noleta brought by a tuna casserole. I refrigerated it. She was real worried this was gonna affect y'all's friendship. She kicked G.W. out. I give her a Valium.

LA VONDA. That's sweet.

LATRELLE. So, it's true?

LA VONDA. Of course it's true. There's a police record on it and everything. Why wouldn't you think it was true? *(Then to SISSY.)* This ain't gonna affect our friendship.

SISSY. I told 'er that. But you oughta go by and see her. She's real upset.

LATRELLE. I just can't believe it. Did they arrest G.W.?

(LA VONDA crosses to the couch, sits and eats her food, while smoking.)

LA VONDA. For what? Leavin' two wooden legs in the wrong place? No, they just had to investigate, you know, given the circumstances. I read the coroner's report. Mama hit her head on the sink and the blow caused her brain to be flooded with blood and she internally hemorrhaged to death.

SISSY. Bless her heart.

LATRELLE. *(Gasps.)* Oh...

(LATRELLE sits on the chair by the couch and cries.)

LA VONDA. They say she never suffered.

(SISSY crosses and joins LA VONDA on the couch.)

SISSY. Well, I just think that Sister just felt so cooped up all those years with your Daddy. You know how he was. She just, you know, had needs.

LATRELLE. Needs?

LA VONDA. Yes, needs, Latrelle. Some of us have needs. It runs in this family. Although, I'm quite convinced it musta skipped a gene or something when you was born.

LATRELLE. I have needs too, I'll have you know. I just don't make them public. My needs are kept in the privacy of my own bedroom!

SISSY. Well, I don't recall any of mine being made in a public place, Latrelle.

LAVONDA. *(Suggestively.)* Unfortunately, I can't say the same.

SISSY. *(Laughing.)* Oh, you are awful.

LA VONDA. Guilty.

(SISSY'S cigarette cough returns as they share a laugh.)

LATRELLE. Our one and only Mama has died by tripping over two wooden legs and hitting her head on the sink of a seedy motel room where she was committing adultery! And you all are laughing! Well, I don't think it's funny!

SISSY. Oh, Latrelle...

LATRELLE. No! *(Rises.)* Just leave me alone! I thought you were gonna back me on this!

SISSY. I'm sorry, hon. But, you know, I believe that all these decisions should be made by Sister's kids. I just decided that. Just decided it right this very minute on the spot.

LATRELLE. Fine. Well, since, I'm the oldest, then I should be in charge and I should make all major decisions.

LA VONDA. Bullshit! We should all get an equal vote. Sissy you should get a vote too. You've always been more like a sister than an aunt to us.

SISSY. I don't really want a vote.

LA VONDA. And Brother Boy should vote too. Of course, it's hard to vote when you're locked up in a looney bin.

SISSY. Cain't argue with that.

LATRELLE. Would you stop?! I have enough on my mind without you bringing up Brother Boy.

SISSY. Brother Boy thought he was Tammy Wynette the last time I seen him. About a year ago.

LA VONDA. Before that it was Loretta.

SISSY. Didn't he do Kitty Wells too way back when?

LA VONDA. Oh, God, I'd forgotten that. "It Wasn't God Who Made Honky Tonk Angels." Umm, mm, mmm. That's a good song. Someone oughta re-do that 'un. I believe Trisha Yearwood could just sing the shit outta that one.

LATRELLE. Do you eat with that mouth too?

LA VONDA. Mostly.

(LA VONDA takes a big bite of fried chicken.)

SISSY. Loretta was always my favorite, though. I swear in that get-up, and that big ol' white gown, Brother Boy was her spittin' image.

LA VONDA. Sissy Spacek couldn't hold a candle to Brother Boy's Loretta.

SISSY. No, she could not. When he pretended to sing along to her records, you almost forgot. Lord, he could tear up, "You Ain't Woman Enough To Take My Man!"

LATRELLE. Who cares!

LA VONDA. Me and Sissy.

LATRELLE. Why?!

LA VONDA. 'Cause he's my baby brother, Latrelle. And I want to get him out.

LATRELLE and SISSY. Out!?

LATRELLE. Did you say out!?

LA VONDA. Yes, out. I called the institution this mornin'.

LATRELLE. You what?

SISSY. *(Overlap.)* You called 'em?

LA VONDA. Called 'em. He needs to know about Mama. And they said now that Mama's dead, you and me are responsible. And if we sign the proper papers, we can get Brother Boy out. He can live with me. I just thank he should be here for his own Mama's funeral.

SISSY. I think LaVonda may be right.

LATRELLE. Well I don't! We can't have Brother Boy at the funeral. He'd be a spectacle. Mama's death is enough of an embarrassment without having Brother Boy at the funeral. Besides, in case you're forgetting, LaVonda—he's crazy!

LA VONDA. Brother Boy is not crazy!

LATRELLE. *(Points to head.)* There's something wrong with him up here and you know it!

SISSY. I'm not sure what's wrong with him is up there.

(LA VONDA lights another cigarette. SISSY watches her every drag.)

LA VONDA. The only thing wrong with him—if it's wrong—is he likes to dress up like a woman.

LATRELLE. That's wrong!

LA VONDA. According to who, Latrelle?!

LATRELLE. According to the Bible! According to God!

SISSY. *(Rises.)* Off and runnin'.

LA VONDA. You mean to tell me that there's a scripture that says, "Men shalt not dress up in women's clothes?"

SISSY. Y'all...

LA VONDA. Maybe you're the crazy one, Latrelle.

SISSY. LaVonda!

(SISSY throws her hands up and exits to the kitchen.)

LATRELLE. Hey, I'm not the one who wants to bury a woman in a mink stole in the middle of a heatwave!

LA VONDA. Mama loved that stole, Latrelle.

LATRELLE. Yes, but she had the good fashion sense not to wear it in the summertime! *(Calling out.)* Sissy, say something! I thought you were on my side!

(SISSY charges onstage.)

SISSY. I'm not on anybody's side! I don't care, quite frankly! I am trying to quit smokin'!!!! And the two of you are gettin' on my nerves. And my arm hurts. *(Emotional.)* It don't matter if Sister wears that stole 'cause she's dead and will be buried shortly and ever'body'll forget about it in no time flat anyway! It don't matter! So, hush up! Both of ya!

LA VONDA. *(Long pause.)* You know why she don't want Mama buried in that stole?

SISSY. No, I don't.

(SISSY exits in defeat.)

LA VONDA. *(Calling.)* 'Cause it's an antique and it's valuable. And that stole is in real good shape.

LATRELLE. Oh please!

LA VONDA. Don't try to deny it, Latrelle, although that's your speciality if I'm not mistaken. Denial!

LATRELLE. What are you talking about denial? Denial about what?

LA VONDA. About everything! About how Mama died, about why you want to keep Brother Boy cooped up like some damn animal.

LATRELLE. And why is that, pray tell?

LA VONDA. *(Takes a drag, then.)* Nevermind.

LATRELLE. No, I want to hear this!

LA VONDA. Look, all I'm sayin' is that, well, you know how close me and Ty are—

LATRELLE. Don't you dare bring my son into this sordid picture. What does my son have to do with this?!

LA VONDA. I'm just saying that Ty has more in common with Brother Boy than you're willin' to admit!

SISSY. *(Re-enters.)* Oh Lord.

LA VONDA. And I think you blame Brother Boy for the way Ty is.

LATRELLE. Ty isn't anything, so you just shut your mouth about my son, LaVonda!

LA VONDA. I went up to New York to see a play he was in.

LATRELLE. What?!

LA VONDA. I went up to New York to see "Staccato." Openin' night. And he was real good. Sissy, the play was spectacular...very senchus with a powerful message. And I went out afterward with Ty and the *all male* cast. And we went to an *all male* bar. And that's when he told me that—

LATRELLE. *(Angry emotion.)* My son is NOT a homosexual!!!! So you just shut up! Shut the hell up 'cause I do not want to hear this!

LA VONDA. You're in denial, Latrelle.

LATRELLE. I am not in denial!!! Quit sayin' I'm in denial!!! I am not in denial!!!!

LA VONDA. (Overlap.) Okay, I'll quit sayin' it, but it ain't gonna change the truth. And the truth is—

LATRELLE. I DON'T WANT TO HEAR THE TRUTH, LA VONDA!!!! Did you ever think that I don't want to know the truth?

(Silence. A stand-off. LATRELLE then bursts into tears and sinks on the couch. Lights start to dim. SISSY walks towards LATRELLE, considers comforting her, then changes her mind, grabs LA VONDA's cigarettes and walks over to the door. She takes one, lights it and takes a long drag, staring hard at LA VONDA.)

LA VONDA. *(Mutters.)* Sh...

(LA VONDA stares at SISSY, then back at LATRELLE. The anger drains from her face and she walks over to her sister, sits next to her, puts her arm around her and cradles her. Her face fills with emotion as LATRELLE buries her head on LA VONDA's shoulder and sobs.)

LA VONDA. *(cont.)* Shh. It's okay. It's okay. I'm sorry. Shh.

(Lights fade to Black, except for a special around SISSY at the doorway.)

SISSY. *(Distant.)* I'da never quit smokin' if I'd known Sister was gonna die.

(Lights Dim to Blackout, leaving only the glow of SISSY's ciga-rette.)

END OF CHAPTER ONE

CHAPTER TWO

Two Wooden Legs

(A guitar strum in the darkness. A Spotlight hits BITSY MAE who is standing in the theatre aisle, leaning against the wall. [Note: While BITSY sings, onstage the cast and crew strike the set and set up the next one])

BITSY.
"O they tell me of a home far beyond the skies,
O they tell me of a home far away;
O they tell me of a home where no storm-clouds rise,
O they tell me of an uncloudy day.

O the land of cloudless day,
O the land of an uncloudy day;
O they tell me of a home where no storm-clouds rise,
O they tell me of an uncloudy day.

O they tell me that He smiles on His children there,
And His smile drives their sorrow all away;
And they tell me that no tears ever come again,
In that lovely land of uncloudy day.

O the land of cloudless day,
O the land of an uncloudy day;
O they tell me of a home where no storm-clouds rise,
O they tell me of an uncloudy day.

(Key change, dramatic and soulful)

O the land of cloudless day,
O the land of an uncloudy day;
O they tell me of a home where no storm-clouds rise,
O they tell me of an uncloudy day."

(The spotlight fades. BITSY exits. Lights come up on TY sitting in his chair downstage center talking to his therapist again.)

TY. When I was a kid, I was fat. A fat boy. Waddlebutt. That's what the other kids called me. I wish they could see my ass today. I've worked really hard on my ass. *(Realizes.)* Anyway. One year—I think I was in fifth grade—my Mama took me shopping for school clothes and I had gotten fatter and I had to try on jeans and the only ones that would fit were the "Husky" ones. And they had this label on the back that said, "Husky!" Kinda announced to everyone behind you that you were a "Husky!" And I started crying. Because I didn't want the other kids to know I was a "Husky." So, my Mama sat me down right there in the store, hugged me and told me that no one ever had to know. Just me and her. Our little secret. And she bought me those "Husky" jeans, took them home. Went to the Goodwill and bought some used jeans, took the labels off the "Husky" ones and she sewed on "Slim" labels from the Goodwill ones. "Slim." Shit. Like I could pull that off. *(Laughs, then mood change.)* But that's the kind of Mama she was. She never made me feel bad about being fat. Always made it okay. And

I've always thought that was unconditional love and maybe if I told her I was gay it'd, you know, apply. But there's this other thought that keeps running through my head—that she'd try and change the labels. You know, instead of from "Husky" to "Slim", from gay to straight, so no one would know. I mean, I tried to do that for years.

(Lights dim to Blackout as a country song plays loudly. Lights come up to reveal G. W. NETHERCOTT late 40's, rugged, a man's man, standing in despair by the jukebox in Bubba's Beer Joint. TY's chair is moved and is sitting at a round bar table, downstage center, where ODELL OWENS, 40's, performs string tricks like Jacob's ladder, cat's cradle, cup 'n saucer etc., singing along to the song. His brother, WARDELL "BUBBA" OWENS, late 40's, the proprietor here, wipes down the bar, also singing. There are two bar stools in front of the bar. The song ends and G. W. crosses to the table.)

ODELL. That's a good un'.
WARDELL. Real good.
G.W. Not since Nam. No, sir. Not since Nam. Shit.

(G.W. sits as WARDELL crosses, handing him a fresh beer.)

WARDELL. Here ya go, G.W.

(WARDELL pats G.W. on the back.)

G.W. I just can't get'er off my mind, Wardell.
WARDELL. Well, that's some serious-ass shit you been through, boy.
G.W. I'm in agony.
WARDELL. I can tell.

G.W. I'm in hell.

ODELL. *(Showing his latest string accomplishment.)* Jacob's ladder. *(Takes a piece of string with his mouth and pulls.)* Witch's hat. You do Jacob's ladder, then witch's hat. Two tricks in one. Well, one trick. Then another by just pullin' the string with ya teeth. Ain't that neat?

G. W. You have too much time on your hands, Odell.

ODELL. *(Oblivious, starts another trick.)* You know what I can't get offa my mind?

WARDELL. Oh boy, here we go again.

ODELL. I can't get that pig bloatin' incident offa my mind.

G.W. What?

WARDELL. G.W., please. If I have to hear about that god-damn pig one more time, I think I'll just shit!

ODELL. It all happened over at the Tyler County Fair.

WARDELL. Well, now's just as good a time as any. *(He grabs a newspaper from the bar and exits to the bathroom.)* Y'all keep an eye on the place.

ODELL. Sure thang, Bubba. See, I go down to Tyler ever' year for the County Fair. *(Showing another string trick.)* Broom. I just love all the animals and the displays of macrame and the cookin' competition and all. 'Sides it gives me a chance to see me and Wardell's sister.

G.W. How is ol' Mozelle?

ODELL. Oh, she's fine.

G.W. You know, me and Mozelle—we had us some good times once upon a time.

ODELL. You know her and Darrel have had a buncha marital problems. He beat her up a few times, but after me and Wardell went over there and showed him what a good ass-whoopin' was all about, he's been a perfect husband and father ever since. You know how Bubba feels about his little sister. *(Showing another string trick.)* Teepee.

G.W. Well, I never though that Darrel Koontz never was worth a good goddamn anyhow. Any man who beats a woman is no man at all.

ODELL. He's in group therapy for abusive husbands now. A buncha wife beaters gets together onced a week with this specialist in wife beatin' and they purge. Some of 'em are dead-beat dads too. There used to be two groups, one for wife beaters and one for dead-beat dads, but so many crossed over from one group to the next, that they merged. *(Thinks.)* Hey, they merged and they purged.

G.W. Purged?

ODELL. Uh-huh. That's when you all kinda spew forth your story and then you feel better after'n you spew forth. Darrel says it works. Hadn't laid a hand on Mozelle since he started purgin'. Said it disgusts him now. 'Course I think that whoppin' mighta had somethin' to do with it.

G.W. Well, I probably shoulda married Mozelle instead of Noleta, then maybe I wouldn't been compelled to fool around and Peggy woulda still been alive. Life is a big ol' pile of shit, Odell.

ODELL. You know G.W., no offense, but you're startin' to get on my nerves. I mean, get off the cross, buddy—we need the wood! *(Pause.)* That was a joke, G.W. You know, to lift your spirits.

G.W. Uh-huh. Well you of all people have a lot of gall to say that I'm gettin' on your nerves when you stay on ever'body's nerves about 99.9 percent of the goddamn time!

ODELL. I'll have you know, a lotta people find me to be a very interesting person.

G.W. Who?

ODELL. Vera Lisso over at the Piggly Wiggly.

G.W. Bullshit.

ODELL. Why when I told her my pig story, she was absolutely riveted!

G.W. That's 'cause she can't get up!!

ODELL. *(Turns away.)* You've done gone and hurt my feelings now.

(ODELL pouts.)

G.W. Okay, Odell, I'm sorry. Go ahead, tell me your pig story.

ODELL. Nun-uh. Ain't gonna tell it.

G.W. Oh, come on.

ODELL. I'm gonna save it for someone who really wants to hear it.

G.W. Just tell it. Don't be a baby.

ODELL. Nope. Ain't gonna do it.

G.W. Alright, fine, suit yourself. I don't give a shit.

ODELL. *(Pause.)* It all happened at the swine weigh-in.

G.W. The swine weigh-in?

ODELL. You know, where they weigh the hogs to make sure they qualify for the competition. They have to meet these Future Farmer's of America guidelines, you know.

G.W. Ah ha.

ODELL. Well, this one kid was told that his pig was a few pounds light and wouldn't get to compete unless it gained a few pounds right quick like.

G.W. Uh-huh.

ODELL. *(Finishes another string trick.)* Cup-in-saucer. Pocket book. Two tricks in one. Didn't even use my teeth. Ain't that neat.

G.W. *(Angrily grabs the string, wads it up and throws it on the floor.)* What happened to the pig, Odell?

ODELL. I'm gettin' to that, G.W. *(He takes another string out of his pocket.)* Well, as I rounded the corner to where they was all lined up for the porta potty, that's when I witnessed the whole she-bang. That kid and a bunch of his buddies. They all looked like juvenile delinquents to me. They was holding that pig down while they was sticking a garden hose and puttin' water down that poor ol' pig's throat. Well, I yelled out, "Hey what you boys doin' to that pig?" And the biggest one said "Don't you never mind. This here's my pig. Just go drain ya pipe." Told me to go drain my pipe. Well, about that time *(Chokes up again.)* I'm sorry, but the vision—it haunts me, G.W.

WARDELL. *(Re-enters.)* You mean to tell me, you ain't finished?

ODELL. I got sidetracked.

WARDELL. Naw!

ODELL. Shut up, Wardell.

WARDELL. Don't you tell me to shut up or I'll whoop your ass!

ODELL. Go to hell, Wardell!

WARDELL. Lead the way!

ODELL. *(Back to G.W.)* So, I started to go on my way and just forget about the whole thang when that poor ol' pig fell over, start-ed wallerin' around and convulsin', then...*(Close to tears.)*...it just lay down and...and—

WARDELL. Died. The damn pig died! Kaput! Done! Finished! End of story. *Next!*

ODELL. Didn't even get to compete in the fair.

WARDELL. Yeah, well that's a damn shame. But I guess now that life can go on, huh, G.W?

G.W. Except for the pig's.

(G.W. starts laughing.)

WARDELL. *(Joins in.)* Except for the pig's. Goddamn! That's a good 'un.

ODELL. Well, it's not funny!

WARDELL. Oh, yeah it is. That's the first time G.W.'s laughed since Peggy died.

(G.W. suddenly stops laughing and begins to cry.)

G.W. Shit... shit...

ODELL. *(Pats G.W. on the shoulder.)* It's okay, buddy. I know how you feel, G.W. I still have nightmares over that pig myself... with water spewin' out of it's nose and snout—

G.W. *(Exploding.)* I don't give a shit about that filthy, dirty, slop-eating, mud-wallerin' pig, Odell! I have killed a woman by irresponsibly leaving these legs in the middle of the motel room after we made long passionate love.

WARDELL. Oh my Lord.

G.W. And I haven't killed a person since Nam. And I didn't love any of them slant-eyed gooks. And killin' them has haunted me for years. So how am I s'pose to go on after killin' someone I love? Huh? You'll get over that pig, Odell. I ain't ever gonna get over killin' Peggy.

WARDELL. G.W., go easy on yourself, buddy. She tripped on your legs on her way to the bathroom. It's not your fault. It was an accident. Coulda happened to anyone.

ODELL. Anyone with two wooden legs, you mean.

WARDELL. Shut up, Odell!

ODELL. Go to hell, Wardell!!

WARDELL. Lead the way!!!

(Pause. ODELL starts doing another trick.)

ODELL. I'll tell you another thing I can't get offa my mind—

WARDELL. Oh, shit.

ODELL. That Ebola virus...

WARDELL. I swear to Christ, if you go into that one again, I'll beat you half to death.

ODELL. It all started in Zaire—

(NOLETA and LA VONDA storm in. They are both drunk and NOLETA brandishes a pistol, while LA VONDA is waving a shotgun. They have obviously given each other make-overs and wear sunglasses.)

NOLETA. Put your hands over your heads and don't make any sudden moves!

LA VONDA. *(Overlap.)* Now! Move it!

WARDELL. Shit...!

(ODELL quickly throws his hands over his head, G.W. and WARDELL just stare at the women for a moment.)

G.W. What the hell do you think you're doin', woman?

NOLETA. We just watched "Thelma and Louise" and we're pissed.

LA VONDA. At men.

NOLETA. All men! Especially the three of y'all.

ODELL. Why are you pissed at me? What did I ever do?

NOLETA. You live and breathe, Odell, so just shut up and quit askin' questions. We'll ask the questions, okay?!

ODELL. Okay.

NOLETA. You make me sick, G.W. Just looking at ya makes me wanna kill ya dead!

G.W. C'mon, Noleta—

NOLETA. It's Thelma!

LA VONDA. I thought I was Thelma.

NOLETA. No, Thelma's the one with the shitty husband. Hey, I said hands up, G.W.! You too, Wardell. Now!!! I mean it.

WARDELL. Okay, okay.

LA VONDA. Why, hello, Wardell.

WARDELL. Hey, LaVonda. You're lookin' good.

LA VONDA. Yeah, well, I work at it. So, you and your nitwit brother over there beat up any queers lately?

ODELL. Hey! I ain't no nit-wit.

LA VONDA. LIAR!!!

G.W. Y'all are drunk.

NOLETA. No shit. And I'm on Valium, too. You have no idea how much I hate your stinkin' guts right now, G.W.

G.W. Noleta, come on, we can talk about this—

NOLETA. *(Smacks him up side the head.)* Shut up!

G.W. Ow!

WARDELL. LaVonda, you know I've always felt real bad over that incident with Brother Boy.

LA VONDA. You feel bad, huh? He feels bad.

NOLETA. Bad.

LA VONDA. You feel bad and he's rottin' in a crazy farm because of you! Big deal, Wardell! It's time to get even!

WARDELL. But that happened over twenty years ago.

LA VONDA. I don't want to hear it, Wardell, so just shut the hell up! *(She pumps the shotgun.)* And I mean it!

WARDELL. Okay, okay, just don't shoot.

ODELL. I don't like this.

G.W. *(Laughs, to WARDELL.)* I don't know why you're over there peein' in your Wranglers. Them guns ain't loaded and even if they was, they wouldn't have the gumption to shoot.

NOLETA. Wanna bet!? *(She shoots across the room and some bull horns fall.)* Whooeee! In the words of Thelma, I thank I've got a knack for this shit.

LA VONDA. You sure do. Nice shot, Thelma.

NOLETA. Thanks, Louise, but I was aimin' for his head.

G.W. Noleta, now come on—

NOLETA. It's THELMA, you shithead!!!

G.W. Okay, okay, Thelma, then. Look, I know I messed up, but you gotta know that I wasn't exactly gettin' what a man needs at home.

NOLETA. What?!!

LA VONDA. Uh-oh.

NOLETA. I hope you ain't gonna try and justify your actions, G.W., 'cause buddy boy, you ain't got a leg to stand on.

LA VONDA. Except them wooden ones.

(LA VONDA laughs.)

NOLETA. Except them wooden ones. That's funny.

(NOLETA laughs.)

G.W. Goddamn! This is worse than Nam.

NOLETA. Hey, Wardell! Get me a shooter! 'Cause I'm startin' to get happy here and we cain't let that happen.

WARDELL. God forbid.

(WARDELL pours a shooter.)

LA VONDA. Get me one too, Wardell.

(WARDELL pours another.)

G.W. For God's sake, woman, c'mon —

NOLETA. Shut up! Until I say otherwise! 'Cause I have somethin' *I* gotta say.

(NOLETA crosses to bar, she and LA VONDA clink glasses, then down shooters.)

NOLETA. *(To WARDELL.)* Thank you. *(Back to G.W.)* Why'd you do it? *(G.W. starts to say something.)* Don't answer that! Just think about it. Do you know what it means to be humiliated, G. W.? Don't answer that! Just think about it. Well, I do. I can't even go out in my own hometown now because everyone knows. Everybody pointin' and whisperin'. "There she is." "Poor pitiful thang." "Bless her heart." God! White trash even feel sorry for me!

LA VONDA. That's true. That is very very true.

NOLETA. Everyone knows that you were carrying on with my best friend's mother. That coulda ruined me and LaVonda's friendship, you know. Did you think of that? Don't answer that! Just think about it. But it didn't. And you wanna know why? Because we're big enough not to let it.

G.W. *(Mumbles.)* You got that right.

LA VONDA. Oooh-he shouldn'ta said that.

NOLETA. What'd you say?!

G.W. I said y'all're certainly big enough. Why do you think I did it, huh? You got as big as a barn and who the hell wants to climb that mountain?

NOLETA. That's it! Take off your shirt!

G.W. What?

NOLETA. I said, take off your shirt!! NOW!!!

(NOLETA puts the pistol right to G.W.'s head.)

G.W. Jesus! Okay, okay.

(G.W. gets up and starts taking off his shirt.)

LA VONDA. *(Waving the shotgun at ODELL and WARDELL.)* You too, boys. Take off ya shirts.

WARDELL. *(Starts to take his off.)* What're y'all doin'?

LA VONDA. Getting even! Odell? What the hell you waitin' for? Christmas?!

ODELL. Okay, Okay.

(ODELL starts taking off his shirt.)

G.W. This is ridiculous.

NOLETA. Ridiculous? I'll tell you what's ridiculous. It's ridiculous for you to bitch about my weight when you look like you're six months pregnant. *(She pokes his stomach with the pistol.)* Look at that gut, LaVonda.

LA VONDA. *(Evaluates.)* Lord! It's time to butcher that hog!

NOLETA. I raised your kids, G.W. I stayed as faithful as the day is long. Cooked ya supper ever' night. And you just shit all over our weddin' vows. Just shit all over 'em. *(To LA VONDA.)* I tried to lose weight. I went to Jenny Craig's and lost twenty-two pounds. *(Smacks and screams at ODELL.)* Twenty-two goddamn pounds! And he never even noticed. Never said one word.

G.W. Yeah, well, that'd be kinda like the Titanic losin' a couple deck chairs.

LA VONDA. You really are a shit, G.W. I wonder what my Mama saw in your sorry ass, anyway?

NOLETA. Off with your pants, G.W.

G.W. Wha...I ain't gonna—

NOLETA. TAKE OFF YOUR GODDAMN PANTS, ASS-HOLE!!!

(NOLETA fires the gun. A piece of ceiling comes crashing down.)

G.W. *(Taking them off.)* Jesus...God...damn...shit...!!

LA VONDA. You too, boys, Quit ya grinnin' and drop ya linen.

WARDELL. Oh, man. What did I do to deserve this?

LA VONDA. You ruined my brother's life, Wardell. Along with your nitwit brother there. So, take 'em off!!!

(The brothers start taking off their pants.)

ODELL. I don't much appreciate you callin' me a nitwit.

LA VONDA. Fine. How about half-wit?

ODELL. I don't like that either.

G.W. *(Throws pants on the floor.)* There! Are ya satisfied?

NOLETA. You ain't satisfied me in years.

LA VONDA. I loved you, Wardell, but you had to ruin it all by beating the shit outta Brother Boy.

WARDELL. I beat the shit outta him because you said he was in love with me.

LA VONDA. You know what Mama said the day the sheriff brought Brother Boy home all beat to a bloody pulp? *(Waving gun at ODELL.)* Huh? Do you?!

ODELL. *(Scared shitless.)* No, I don't.

LA VONDA. She said, "Well, that just proves my point. He just can't live in regular society like a normal human bein'. It's too dangerous." *(Emotional.)* And the very next day, her and Daddy drove him over to Big Springs and signed the papers for him to rot in that crazy farm. *(Drops emotion, intense anger.)* And I will never forgive you for that, Wardell! And I'll never forgive myself for tellin' you he was in love with you. You ruined his life, Wardell!

WARDELL. You think I don't think about that ever' day of my life? Huh? I thought the world and all of Brother Boy. Loved him like my very own brother. Hell, more than this idiot.

(WARDELL indicates ODELL.)

ODELL. You loved that queer more than me?

WARDELL. Brother Boy was my first friend. My best friend. And when he turned queer, it liked to killed me. I just felt so betrayed. But I never meant to hurt him, Vonie. I just lost it when you told me that. I flipped out.

ODELL. I flipped out, too!

WARDELL. I'm sorry, LaVonda. But can I please get dressed? I mean, what if someone walked in? This is a place of business for cryin' out loud.

(WARDELL starts to put on his pants. LA VONDA snatches them with the shotgun barrel and flings them across the bar.)

LA VONDA. Tough titty!

NOLETA. Hey Louise, you wanna take the pictures or hold the gun?

G.W. Pictures?

LA VONDA. I guess I'll hold the gun. *(Stares at WARDELL's crotch.)* Since mine's bigger.

NOLETA. Okay.

(NOLETA starts digging around in her purse, pulls out a black lacy bra and throws it at G.W.)

NOLETA. Here, titty man. Put this on.

G.W. *(Catching it.)* What?! I ain't puttin' on...You can't be serious—

(NOLETA fires her pistol in the air.)

G.W. Damn...

WARDELL. *(Overlap.)* Shit...

ODELL. *(Overlap.)* Ahhhh!!!

WARDELL. Just put on the brassiere, G.W.!

G.W. Fine. Fine! *(Glaring at NOLETA as he puts it on.)* You are one mean-ass bitch!

NOLETA. You're just lucky I ain't Latin and got a butcher knife.

G.W. *(Struggling with hooking bra.)* Shit...

LA VONDA. Help 'im with the hooks, Wardell. I know you know how to do that. At least you know how to undo 'em. *(Cattle prodding him with shotgun over to G.W.)* Quit pussy footin' around! Now c'mon! Hook 'em!

WARDELL. *(Hooking up G.W.)* Okay, okay...shit!

ODELL. *(Laughing.)* You oughta see yourself, G. W. Damn... *(Laughs more.)* Thank God I don't have a mean-ass bitch wife, too.

NOLETA. *(Turning.)* What did you say?

ODELL. I take it back!

NOLETA. Too late! Sit your ass down.

(NOLETA pushes him in a chair, then starts digging through her bag and pulls out some earrings and a turban and hands them to LaVonda, then pulls out a handful of makeup.)

NOLETA. *(To LA VONDA, indicating WARDELL.)* These are for him.

(NOLETA hands her pistol to LA VONDA, who sticks it in her jeans, so she can make-over ODELL.)

ODELL. Please! LaVonda, I'm sorry about that Brother Boy incident. Wardell made me—

LA VONDA. Hush up, Pauline Pitiful.

NOLETA. *(To ODELL.)* Pucker up.

(ODELL does. NOLETA smears lipstick on his lips.)

LA VONDA. *(Hands earrings to WARDELL.)* Here, put these on.

WARDELL. This ain't right, LaVonda.

NOLETA. *(To ODELL.)* Okay, go like this. *(She presses her lips together, then smacks, ODELL complies.)* Nice. That's Misty Rose from Avon. Just in case you like it, you'll know. Good color on you. *(As she paints ODELL's eyebrows, laughing, mumbles.)* Pauline Pitiful. *(To LA VONDA.)* That's funny.

LA VONDA. *(Evaluating WARDELL's earrings.)* What'daya think, Thelma?

NOLETA. Oh yeah, nice. Turban.

LA VONDA. *(Hands the turban to WARDELL.)* Put this on. *(Spots G.W.'s wooden legs across the bar, crosses, stalking him.)* So, those are the culprits that killed my Mama.

(LA VONDA bangs the legs with the shotgun.)

G.W. Hey, I'm a veteran, goddamnit!

LA VONDA. *(Re: turban.)* Oh, turn that around, Wardell. The jewel goes in front.

WARDELL. Oh.

(WARDELL complies. NOLETA finishes ODELL by clipping a poofy red flower in his hair. She turns the severely painted face towards LA VONDA.)

NOLETA. What'daya think, Louise?

LA VONDA. *(Evaluates.)* That is one ugly bitch!

NOLETA. Okay. Odell, go sit over there. *(Points to a bar stool.)* Wardell come on outta there and sit on this bar stool. *(WARDELL complies.)* It's time for a group picture.

(She hands her pistol to LA VONDA, so she can make-over ODELL.)

G.W. I'm beggin' you, baby.

NOLETA. Save it for someone who gives a shit! Now get on over there with your boyfriends and give 'em a group hug. Come on! Now! Before I make ya do somethin' even more humiliatin'. I'm starting to get pissed again!

(G.W. takes his place between the brothers. NOLETA snaps a picture, pulls it out and places it on the table.)

LA VONDA. *(Waving the gun.)* Y'all can do better than that! Put ya arms around each other. Act like you love one another.

(G.W., ODELL, WARDELL comply.)

NOLETA. *(Snapping another picture, puts it on the table.)* Now, G. W, look in Wardell's eyes longingly like you did with that tramp you cheated on me with.

LA VONDA. Hey, that was my mama!

NOLETA. Sorry. Do it, G. W.! *(He makes a feeble attempt, she snaps a picture and lays it on the table.)* Now say, "I love you, Wardell!"

G.W. Ain't no way—

(LA VONDA fires the pistol.)

G.W. *(Quickly.)* I love you, Wardell!

NOLETA. That's more like it. *(Glances at the pictures "developing" on the table.)* Oh, these are looking good.

LA VONDA. They sure are.

G.W. Shit. Are we done yet?

NOLETA. Almost. Just as soon as you reach over and kiss Odell. On the mouth!

G.W. Okay, that's it!

(G.W. crosses to LA VONDA, grabs the gun and sticks it to his head, LA VONDA still holding it.)

G.W. Go ahead. Shoot me! Just kill me dead right here and now 'cause I'll be goddamn if I'm gonna kiss Odell!

WARDELL. *(Losing it.)* Oh, shut up, G.W., and take your punishment like a man!

G.W. Like a man? Like a man? Well, that's a little hard to do, Wardell—WHILE WEARING A BLACK BRASSIERE!!!

WARDELL. Yeah, well, you made your bed, so just by gawd lay in it! And maybe she's doin' you a favor. Did you think about that? Huh?

G.W. A favor? What the hell are you talkin' about? A favor.

WARDELL. All I'm saying is that at least she's getting even right after it happened. I beat the shit outta my homo best friend and sent him packing to the loony bin for the rest of his life. And I have been livin' with that guilt for twenty some odd years now! *(To LA VONDA.)* I wish you had done this sooner. Then maybe my life woulda been better than this. *(Back to G.W.)* So, maybe your life's gonna be better, G.W., by wearing that perty little lacy black brassiere. That's all I'm sayin'. What can I do, LaVonda? What can I do to make it better? What can I do for you? What can I do for Brother Boy? *(Emotional.)* Maybe I can do somethin', LaVonda. Just tell me what I can do.

LA VONDA. *(Softly.)* Ain't nothin' you can do, Wardell. Not now.

(LA VONDA pats WARDELL on the back with the pistol.)

WARDELL. I am so sorry.

LA VONDA. I just wish Brother Boy knew.

WARDELL. Me too.

LA VONDA. *(Composing herself.)* Well, I think we've done some good here today. I feel like I been to church.

NOLETA. *(Re: pictures.)* These are nice. Don't ever let anybody tell you boys you ain't photogenic.

ODELL. What you gonna do with them pictures, Thelma?

NOLETA. Sell 'em, asshole, what the hell do you think?!

ODELL. What are you gonna do with all our stuff, Louise?

LA VONDA. Burn it, Pauline! *(Re: jukebox.)* Oh, here's a good 'un.

(LA VONDA makes her selection and the music begins.)

NOLETA. G.W., you and Odell—dance. And then we'll be gone.

(G.W. approaches ODELL, they stare at each other.)

G.W. Damn, shit, hell, fire! *(Pause)* I'll be the man.

ODELL. Lookin' like that?

(G.W. grabs ODELL and starts clumsily dancing with him.)

NOLETA. *(A little emotional.)* He never took me dancin'. Not once. And that hurts.

LA VONDA. Men! Okay, Wardell, ask Odell if you can cut in. Go ahead on. It'll ease that guilt.

WARDELL. Then I'll gladly do it. *(Goes over)* Odell.

ODELL. Yeah?

WARDELL. Can I cut in?
ODELL. *(Quickly.)* Sure thang, Wardell.

(ODELL rushes away and sits on stool.)

G.W. Shit...

(WARDELL and G.W. start dancing.)

LA VONDA. I had to do it, Wardell. For Brother Boy.
WARDELL. I'm glad you did. I feel better now.
G.W. Jesus H. Christ!

(The girls put on their sunglasses, NOLETA puts her arm around LA VONDA and turns the camera towards them.)

NOLETA. Hey, Louise.
LA VONDA. Yeah, Thelma.

(NOLETA takes the classic "Thelma & Louise" picture.)

NOLETA. Let's go on over to Tiny's Liquor and stick him up. He shortchanged me the other day.
LA VONDA. Why that son-of-a-bitch. Let's go!

(NOLETA and LA VONDA exit as lights start to dim, leaving WARDELL and G.W. only in a Spotlight as the music continues. WARDELL and G.W. continue to dance a couple of moments, then WARDELL lays his head on G.W.'s shoulder.)

WARDELL. I shoulda never beat up Brother Boy.

(Blackout.)

END OF CHAPTER TWO

CHAPTER THREE

The Dehomosexualization of Brother Boy

(A strum of a guitar in the darkness. Then the Spotlight hits BITSY MAE, standing onstage at her mike [like at the beginning of the play]. TY sits in the darkness, but can be seen, very shadowlike from the spotlight leakage. BITSY gives the audience an impish smile and sings:)

BITSY.
"Now when the Lord dips us in the gene pool,
We get more than Granny's green eyes.
We get our Mama's warmth,
Our Daddy's cool, *(She glances at TY.)*
And that thang between our thighs.
And that's the start of all these troubles
In our sordid lives.

Ain't it a bitch sortin' out our sordid lives?
It's a bitch when you come to realize
Crack yerself a box of Cracker Jack,
You could get a really shitty prize!
It's a bitch sortin' out our sorry little
sordid lives!"

(The Spotlight fades. BITSY exits. Lights up on TY in his chair as he continues his therapy.)

TY. My grandmother died yesterday. I don't want to go back to the funeral. I can't be who I am down there. At least here, I can choose to be in places where I can be who I am. Down there, I'll have to butch it up. Oh God, I get so tired of butching it up. Every audition, every meeting. When I was on the soap, I'd do interviews, you know. Press. I did one with this hysterically funny queeny guy from Soap Opera Digest. And I don't know, I let my guard down and started just being—you know, me. And suddenly we were laughing and talking about Barbra Streisand's concert on HBO. How she was dressed. That black dress. That mahogany table with the water on it...she'd drink so...refined. And those nails! This is not a conversation a couple of straight men would be having. And he just leaned over and said, "I'm glad you're one of us." And I looked at him and realized that I had fucked up. So I put it back on. The butch thing and said, "I don't know what you're talking about." And he said, "That's okay. I understand." That's okay. I understand. Well, they *don't* understand down there. My Uncle Brother Boy's in a mental institution for God's sake for being a gay transvestite! Locked up since he was like eighteen. And my grandmother put him there. So it's a little hard to mourn her loss. *(Pause.)* His name was Ben Flack. The guy from Soap Opera Digest. Ben loved our show, so he kinda became, you know, like a friend of the cast. Hung out with us. But he stopped showing up on the set and at stuff and then my friend Bobbie Eves—you know the one who played my fiance, who won the Emmy because they killed me off and she got to play *grief* for six months. Well, Bobbie told me that Ben was sick. He wouldn't let any of us go and see him. So I sent him a card and told him I missed him around, and you know, hoped he was feeling better. *(Pause.)* The meds — they don't work for everyone, you know. *(Pause.)* And he wrote me back and said, "Ty Williamson, you are a beautiful man. So talented, your soul runs deep and you ain't hard on the eyes either. I'm glad I knew you. Love, Ben." I'm glad I knew you. Past tense. Then there was, "P. S. Come out, come out wherever you are—and get *happy*." *(Pause, emotional.)* But I can't. Because I care too much. Especially down there. In Texas. Why do I care? Why the fuck do I care?!

(Lights dim to Black then Full Lights come up on the office of DR. EVE BOLINGER, late 40's, the very attractive, alcoholic over-sexed psychologist of this state mental institution. TY's chair is moved and is part of the office decor, which includes a couch and DR. EVE's "desk" [The round table from SISSY's house and the bar now with a different cloth.] DR. EVE stands by her desk and speaks into a mini tape recorder as she paces, sits, paces some more—occasionally drinking from a sipper cup.)

EVE. Friday, July 24, 1998. Dr. Eve Bolinger. More documentation on the progress of my Dehomosexualization Therapy. Case one. Jose Victor Rodriguez. After three months was able to masturbate to orgasm for the first time while fantasizing about a woman. My belief is that Jose Victor has come from a five to a four and is moving towards a three on the Kinsey scale. Case two—*(Sighs.)* Oh boy. Earl Ingram. AKA Brother Boy. AKA Tammy Wynette. So complicated. The duality of homosexuality and transvestism. This session is...*(Checks notes.)*...number sixty-eight...five times a week...three months...no progress. Today, Earl has promised to arrive with one less item of female attire. No success with masturbation therapy.

(EVE clicks off the tape recorder, then presses intercom.)

EVE. Send him in, please, Ethel.

(She then takes out a compact and checks herself. Satisfied she growls at the mirror)

EVE. Not bad.

(BROTHER BOY enters. 40's. In full make-up and the longest false eyelashes on the market. He wears a pink housecoat, with fuch-sia marabou feathers outlining it. Under the housecoat are women's green pajamas, accessorized with heeled wedgies, adorned with a poof of the same fuchsia feathers as the house-coat. He is wearing a knotted nylon stocking on his head that covers most of his hair. One hand is holding a can of Aqua Net and a cigarette, a purse positioned on that arm. The other hand holds a wig head with a very big poofy blonde wig perched on it, that is partially teased, partially combed out.)

BROTHER BOY. I did it! I did it! I walked right down that hall without my hair on. I feel neked, but I did it. How are you, Dr. Eve?

EVE. Well, good for you, Earl. I'm fine. Sit. Please.

BROTHER BOY. *(Sitting.)* That mean orderly Bumper and some of them other 'uns was catcallin' at me, but I did it. I sure did it.

EVE. Yes, you did! Good for you! I am so proud of you!

BROTHER BOY. Well, thank yewww! *(Indicating wig.)* I washed and set this an hour before my appointment, so it would just have just enough time to dry up under my portable and I wouldn't have time to finish fixing it, so I'd have to bring it to my session to put on the finishin' touches on it bein's I have a show after this in the rec room. I can't disappoint my fans. They're crazy, but they're loyal. They're always there.

EVE. Maybe that's because they're locked up and don't have anywhere else to go. *(Laughs.)* That was a joke.

BROTHER BOY. *(Not amused.)* O-kay.

EVE. I caught your last show.

BROTHER BOY. Oh, well, that 'un was a little bit out of control. Usually I perform after the patients have been medicated. If you could talk to Nurse Jackson and tell her that that was a much better system, I'd sure appreciate it.

EVE. I'll see what I can do. This is a big step, Earl. Very big. You coming in without the wig on. I believe we've made some progress.

(BROTHER BOY digs in his purse, then takes out a fancy rattail comb and proceeds to take the pins and curlers out of the wig and backcomb it.)

BROTHER BOY. Well, I gotta tell you, I feel a little bit like a whore in church.

EVE. You look a little bit like one too. *(Pause.)* That was just another little joke.

BROTHER BOY. *(Attitude.)* O-kay.

EVE. No offense.

BROTHER BOY. None taken. Listen, Dr. Eve, how long is this gonna take?

EVE. It's just a regular session. About forty-five minutes.

BROTHER BOY. No, no, no. This whole dehomosexualization thing. 'Cause it seems to be going at a very slow pace.

EVE. Well, Earl, you really haven't been participating in your own recovery. I don't have a magic wand.

BROTHER BOY. I do. Somewhere back in my room. I've had

it forever. Got it when I was little. Used to pretend I was Glinda the Good Witch. Ordered it from a magaz—

EVE. Earl?

BROTHER BOY. What?

EVE. Could we please stay with our session this time?

BROTHER BOY. So sorry. But you know, I resent...I resent you sayin' that I am not participatin' in my own recovery. I walked right down that hall without my hair on. Came in here lookin' like somethin' the cat drug in.

EVE. Yes, I know. And that's good. But in three months, sixty-eight sessions, this is your very first effort.

BROTHER BOY. Well, I don't like to rush into things. And in my own defense, you did say that I have a severe case of homosexuality.

EVE. It's one of the worst I've ever seen. And with the transvestism, well, it's very very complicated.

BROTHER BOY. *(Testy.)* I am well aware of that, Dr. Eve.

EVE. Now, did you try my masturbation exercises?

BROTHER BOY. *(Still with an attitude.)* Yes, I did.

EVE. And how did that go?

BROTHER BOY. Well, I did just what you asked me. I started masturbating by fantasizing about a man. I used Wardell from back home.

EVE. Of course you did.

BROTHER BOY. Then I switched to a woman.

EVE. Good, good.

BROTHER BOY. At first I couldn't decide who to use. I thought about usin' Tammy Wynette, but that just didn't seem right now that she's...*(Chokes up.)*...gone. That'd just be evil and wrong. I couldn't, you know, think about doing that to her bein's the way I feel about her and all. That'd just be evil and wrong.

EVE. Well, Earl, fantasies are very healthy. And there doesn't have to be anything evil or wrong about sex.

BROTHER BOY. Well, that's not what my mama told me, Missy! *(Chokes up.)* I miss Mama. I hadn't seen my mama now for six months and four days. My sister LaVonda's been visitin' me though.

(He walks over to DR. EVE's "desk" and takes a tissue.)

EVE. Yes, I know. We've had several conversations. And we need to talk about your mama. But not until the end of the session.

BROTHER BOY. LaVonda's wantin' to get me outta here.

EVE. I know that. But you're not ready yet.

BROTHER BOY. Well, when will I be ready?! I've been here for twenty-three years!

EVE. I don't know.

BROTHER BOY. I gotta tell ya, the only thing that's kept me sane has been my career. My country queens. Kitty, Loretta. Then Tammy came along. Lord, I felt like I'd found my soul mate. I followed her rise to the top. And she's had such a rough life. Illness after illness. And George Jones was a drunk, you know. He's a tortured genius. And financial woes. Bought 'erself a buncha shoppin' malls and ever'one of 'em went bellyup. Did you know that Tammy went to Nashville from Mississippi with three little babies in the back seat of her car, honey, they were all under the age of five—

EVE. Earl.

BROTHER BOY. Then they exhumed her.

EVE. Earl!

BROTHER BOY. Whatever happened to "Rest in Peace?" Just dug her up!

EVE. Earl! Please! You always do this. You get extremely sidetracked in our sessions and I truly believe it is so you won't have to face the truth. You are living your life vicariously through

Tammy Wynette and that is just not healthy.

BROTHER BOY. Well, somebody has got to carry on her legacy now that she's...gone.

EVE. Earl, you've been doing this for over twenty years. What was your excuse before she died?

BROTHER BOY. My mind's a blank.

EVE. Well, it has to stop. It's just not healthy!

BROTHER BOY. *(Emotional.)* It gets me through this hell, alright?! Locked up with a buncha looney tunes, like I'm crazy. Tammy Wynette gets me through life, Dr. Eve — and now you're tryin' to take her precious, precious, precious memory away from me and I don't think I can take it.

(He throws himself on the couch and sobs. DR. EVE rushes over with a box of tissues.)

EVE. Oh, here...that's it. Let it out. Let it all out. Crying is good.

BROTHER BOY. Thank you. *(He dabs his eyes.)* Now look what you've done. You've gone and made my mascara run. *(Pause.)* Tammy was a beautician, you know. I've always had a special flair for doing hair, don't you think?

EVE. Could we just keep to our session here?!

BROTHER BOY. Okay.

(He opens his purse, digs around and takes out a tube of mascara, lipstick, and a compact, and proceeds to "freshen up.")

BROTHER BOY. Lord, it is amazin' what a good cry can do for you. When you dehomosexualize me, will I still be able to cry? Because my Daddy always told me that real men don't cry.

EVE. *(Losing her patience.)* I don't know, Earl. We'll cross that bridge if we ever get to it.

BROTHER BOY. I hope you're not givin' up on me. 'Cause I really want to get outta here.

EVE. I'm not. Let's go back to your masturbation exercises, shall we?

BROTHER BOY. Okay. *(Re: wig.)* Do you think this is too poofy?

EVE. *(Testy.)* Maybe.

BROTHER BOY. I mean, she is a country queen. Big hair is important, you know. Did you know that when Tammy was married to George Jones that he onced punched a hole right through—

EVE. Earl!!!

BROTHER BOY. *(Quickly.)* He was drunk.

EVE. EARL!!! My masturbation therapy, okay!?

BROTHER BOY. Okay.

EVE. Now, when you switched to a woman, who did you fantasize about?

BROTHER BOY. You. I masturbated and I fantasized about you.

EVE. Oh...well. Well, well, well. My. Thank you.

BROTHER BOY. Well, actually, it didn't turn out so good. As soon as I switched over to you, now I don't mean to be ugly, but I got kinda nauseous and it...*(Whistles as he does a motion with his finger indicating a penis going flaccid.)*...kinda went South. I'm sorry.

EVE. *(Hurt.)* That's okay. Don't worry about it. So, did you try again?

BROTHER BOY. No, I threw up. So I wasn't in the mood no more. I'm sorry. I'm really sorry. Maybe next time I'll masturbate and think about someone a little more masculine. Oh, oh, oh! I know! What about Miss Jane Hathaway from the Beverly Hillbillies? She's kinda manly.

EVE. *(Getting more frustrated.)* Earl, that's not the point!

BROTHER BOY. Well, I'm sorry. But I'm not quite sure what the point is.

EVE. The point is for you to start fantasizing about a woman! A real woman. A woman who is feminine and sexy and all woman! Not some butch stick of a woman like Miss Jane Hathaway who could be a man in drag for all we know!

BROTHER BOY. Well, I don't know about that. I don't think a man in drag would go out looking that bad. I mean, even when Jethro portrayed Jethrene—

EVE. Augh!!! *(Stands; starts pacing.)* I don't know what to do with you anymore, Earl! I'm at my rope's end! I try and try to make progress and nothing! You are not participating in your own recovery!!!

BROTHER BOY. I'm sorry.

EVE. Do you know what you are doing to me?!

BROTHER BOY. No.

EVE. You are costing me fame and fortune!

BROTHER BOY. I am?

EVE. Yes! I have a book deal pending on my success with you and Jose Victor. Simon and Schuster.

BROTHER BOY. *(Impressed.)* Woo...

EVE. Now Jose Victor is doing very well, but you're not! And you're my ace in the hole, Earl. If I can dehomosexualize you, I can dehomosexualize anyone! That'd mean my theory works and I'd be famous. I'll be on talk shows. Maybe you can come with me.

BROTHER BOY. *("Oh I couldn't.")* Aw, well...

EVE. Does this make any sense whatsoever to you? Do you see where I'm headed?

BROTHER BOY. No, not really.

EVE. I can get out of this god-forsaken state looney bin and have a place in history! That's what I want, Earl, a place in psychological history. Like Freud, Jung. And you are not helping me, Earl. You are not helping me at all!

BROTHER BOY. Well, I tried. I did your masturbation exercises. I can't help it if you don't float my boat! And I walked right down that hall with everyone catcallin' at me, makin' fun, lookin' like a damn fool.

EVE. You always look like a fool, Earl!

BROTHER BOY. Well, that's not very nice.

EVE. Nice? Nice? I don't give a shit about nice, Earl. I want this to work, so I can get the hell out of this shithole and get on Oprah! Is that so complicated? Is that too much to ask for? Can you get that through your head, or has the heat from all the wigs all these years caused some kinda brain damage!?

(She slaps the wig off of the table into BROTHER BOY's lap. He catches it.)

BROTHER BOY. Well, you're startin' to scare me! And I don't particularly care for you calling me a fool. *(Starts to cry.)* Could I have another tissue, please?

(He goes to the box, she beats him to it, snatches it.)

EVE. No! And don't start blubbering again because I am not in the mood.

(She takes the tissue box and puts it on the floor by the chair.)

BROTHER BOY. I just don't consider myself a fool, Dr. Eve. I consider myself a lot of other things, but I do not consider myself a fool!

EVE. Well, you are! What do you think got you here in the first place?! Huh? Walking down that hall today was no different from any other day. People point and laugh at you every day, Earl. Today was no different!

BROTHER BOY. You're startin' to hurt my feelings.

EVE. Yeah? Well, get over it!

(EVE gets up, then an idea hits her. She unbuttons her blouse, tosses it, then kneels down on the couch by BROTHER BOY.)

BROTHER BOY. Dr. Eve, what are you doin'?

EVE. More therapy! *(Coming closer, breasts in his face.)* What are you thinking right now, Earl?

BROTHER BOY. I was wonderin' where you got that bra.

EVE. I want you to fuck me, Earl. Because quite frankly, I think it's time you fuck a woman.

BROTHER BOY. Oh dear sweet Jesus—

EVE. Oh God, it's been so long!!!

(She's on him, trying to unpry his legs.)

BROTHER BOY. *(Overlap.)* I just don't think I can—

EVE. Oh yes you can. Just like that little engine that could, Earl. Say it! "I think I can, I think I can."

BROTHER BOY. *(Shaking his head "no.")* I think I can, I think I can.

EVE. That's it.

BOTH. I think I can.

EVE. Now let's go! FUCK ME!!!!

BROTHER BOY. I don't think I can!

(He gets away. She follows.)

EVE. Oh, yes you can! I can change any man, Earl. Just look at these. Look at 'em.

(She cups her breasts and squeezes them.)

BROTHER BOY. *(Holds his stomach.)* Do you have any Mylanta?

(She positions herself, with her dress hiked, and spreads her legs, one on the chair, the other on the couch — away from the audience.)

EVE. Fuck me, Earl! Fuck me NOW!!!!

(BROTHER BOY screams in horror when he looks up her skirt.)

BROTHER BOY. Dr. Eve! You don't have on any panties!

(He backs against the wall, scared shitless, looks again, screams again, then looks away, holds his stomach and starts taking deep breaths.)

EVE. I know. Now just take yours off and fuck me, Earl!!! FUCK ME!!!

BROTHER BOY. I can't! I'm gonna throw up. I'd throw up all over you. You don't want that. I had enchiladas for lunch. Please, Dr. Eve, I just can't.

EVE. *(Screams in frustration.)* Oh for cryin' out loud, you are just one hopeless pathetic freak. Shit!

(She grabs her jacket and puts it back on as she walks over to her desk.)

BROTHER BOY. *(Crying.)* I'm never gonna get out of here, am I?

(She gets some pills from her purse, a flask, and downs them with a long swig.)

EVE. Shut up! Damn sob sister.

BROTHER BOY. I'm not, am I? I'm not ever gonna get out of here. I can't pass any of your tests. If you can't dehomosexualize me, I'm never gonna get out of here.

(He goes for the tissues, she races across and grabs them.)

EVE. No! You're stuck. Stuck here forever. Just like me. *(She starts laughing.)* Stuck here forever. Like a monkey in the zoo. *(She laughs more.)* Like a goddamn monkey in a goddamn zoo.

(DR. EVE laughs more.)

BROTHER BOY. Um... I don't see anything funny, Dr. Eve.

EVE. Well, I do. *(Continues laughing.)* Oh, by the way, I almost forgot. Your mama died.

BROTHER BOY. What?

EVE. Your mama died.

BROTHER BOY. Mama's dead?

EVE. As a mackerel.

BROTHER BOY. My mama's dead?!

EVE. As a goddamn doornail.

(BROTHER BOY just sits in his chair, stops crying, letting it sink in. EVE continues to swig from the flask, trying not to laugh.)

BROTHER BOY. *(No emotion.)* Oh my god. Mama's dead. My mama's dead. *(To himself.)* I quit cryin'. I'm not even cryin'. My mama's dead and I'm not even sad. Why, Dr. Eve? Why?

EVE. Beats the hell outta me.

(EVE picks up a timer and turns it. It dings.)

EVE. Okay, session's over.

BROTHER BOY. Over? You just tell me my mama's dead. You drop a bombshell like that on me, tell me my mama's dead, then say session's over?

EVE. Hey, I'm beat, okay? You think this is easy? Now get your little monkey ass outta here!

BROTHER BOY. *(Rising.)* Okay.

(He starts gathering up his stuff.)

EVE. And next time please make more of an effort with my masturbation exercises.

BROTHER BOY. Yes, ma'am.

EVE. And show up with no wig and no make-up. It's time you start participating in your...

BOTH. ...own recovery.

BROTHER BOY. I know.

(He starts to exit.)

EVE. Because I'm at my rope's end with you, Earl! Fed up! Understand?!

BROTHER BOY. Yes, ma'am. I'm sorry. I'm so sorry. I'll do my best. *(Pause, stops, then softly.)* No. No, no, no...

EVE. What did you say?

BROTHER BOY. *(Turns back)* I said no! I don't understand! And I'm not gonna do it. Not gonna show up wigless again. Not gonna take off my face. And I'm sure as hell not gonna do those stupid masturbation exercises if I can't masturbate and fantasize about a woman that's manly!

EVE. You will if I say you will!

BROTHER BOY. I won't either! If I'm stuck here, then I'm not doin' nothin' else you say. Nothing! Understand, Dr. Eve?! If I'm stuck in this shithole for the rest of my life, then I am *not* participating in my own recovery! And you can't make me! And if you want to know my opinion, Dr. Eve, you're just a flat-out mean, evil, bitter, alcoholic, sex fiend who needs a lifetime of therapy herself!

EVE. I'M IN THERAPY, YOU LITTLE FAGGOT!!!!

BROTHER BOY. WELL, IT AIN'T A WORKIN'! *(Deep breath, regains his composure.)* Now, if you'll excuse me, I have to go mourn the loss of my mama.

(O.S. We hear a loud commotion, some shots, screaming, etc. DR. EVE and BROTHER BOY run away form the door.)

WARDELL. *(O.S; yelling.)* Okay, everybody just stay calm and nobody'll get hurt.
BROTHER BOY. *(Overlap.)* Oh my Lord! What's happenin'out there?

(WARDELL storms in the room, wearing a cowboy hat, tight Wranglers, looking like a million bucks, holding a gun.)

WARDELL. *(Evaluating.)* Brother Boy?
BROTHER BOY. *(Studies him, then recognizes him.)* Wardell. *(Screaming.)* Ahhhh!!! That's Wardell! *(Turns around, scrambling for the wig.)* No, Wardell. You cain't see me like this! I don't have my hair on and I've cried my face off. Don't look at me, Wardell. I'm not presentable.

(EVE slinks towards WARDELL as BROTHER BOY puts the wig on.)

EVE. *(Sexily.)* So this is Wardell. I've heard a lot about you, Wardell. Dr. Eve Bolinger.

(EVE extends her hand.)

WARDELL. Well, what I need for you to do is go on out there with the others. I'd sure appreciate it, and no one'll get hurt.

(EVE puts her hand on WARDELL's shoulder.)

EVE. Well, I'm not sure I'd mind getting hurt by a big of handsome cowboy like yourself.

(BROTHER BOY bounces up, the wig on, pissed and struts over.)

BROTHER BOY. Back off bitch!

EVE. Excuse me?!

BROTHER BOY. You heard me! Get your damn paws off a him and get the hell on outta here!

EVE. Like I'm scared of you, you little monkey freak!

WARDELL. Hey, hey! Don't you talk to him like that!

BROTHER BOY. Shoot'er, Wardell! Shoot'er in the head!

WARDELL. Now go on. Git.

(WARDELL grabs EVE's arm and pushes her to the door.)

EVE. I like it rough.

BROTHER BOY. Hell, you like it any way you can get it. Now get outta here!

(BROTHER BOY swipes at EVE with his purse, hits the wall.)

WARDELL. Git!

(DR. EVE runs out. WARDELL turns and stares at BROTHER BOY for a long awkward moment.)

WARDELL. Brother Boy.

BROTHER BOY. Wardell.

WARDELL. I am so sorry.

BROTHER BOY. *(Choking up.)* It's okay.

WARDELL. I'll never hurt you again, and I won't let anybody else hurt ya either.

BROTHER BOY. *(Meekly.)* Oh...

WARDELL. I'm takin' you home now.

BROTHER BOY. *(Long pause, chokes up.)* You're takin' me home?

WARDELL. Yes, I am.

BROTHER BOY. *(In tears.)* Oh, thank you, sweet Jesus. I'm goin' home.

(Lights start to Dim as WARDELL grabs BROTHER BOY and they exit.)

WARDELL. All right, we're comin' out, goddamnit!

(He fires the gun, overlapping O. S. screaming. Blackout.)

END OF CHAPTER THREE

CHAPTER FOUR

All Laid Out (In a Mink Stole)

(A guitar strum in the darkness. A Spotlight hits BITSY MAE, who is standing in the theatre aisle — the opposite side as before "Two Wooden Legs" — leaning against the wall. [Note. Again, while BITSY sings, onstage the cast and crew strike the set and set up another one.] By the last chorus, TY should be settled in his chair, seen in the shadows, pensive.)

BITSY.
"I've wandered far away from God,
Now I'm coming home,
The paths of sin too long I've trod.
Lord, I'm coming home.

Coming home. Coming home.
Nevermore to roam.
Open wide thine arms of love.
Lord I'm coming home.

I've wasted many precious years,
Now I'm coming home.
I now repent with bitter tears,
Lord I'm coming home.

71

Coming home, coming home.
Never more to roam
Open wide thine arms of love.
Lord, I'm coming home."

(Key change. BITSY walks up the steps onstage and sings right to
TY — who of course doesn't hear her — emotional, dramatic.)

My soul is sick, my heart is sore,
Now I'm coming home!
My strength renew, my hope restore.
Lord, I'm coming home.

Coming home, Coming home.
Nevermore to roam
Open wide thine arms of love,
Lord I'm coming home.
Open wide thine arms of love.
Lord, I'm coming home."

(The Spotlight fades as she exits. Lights up on TY. Another session.)

TY. I had a great day yesterday! After I left your office, I went
home, laid down on the couch and started drifting. Just letting my
mind float from place to place. And I settled on the soap. And I
thought about my best friend back then. Marc Stein. Great guy.
One of our producers. When I first got on the soap, Marc found out
I played racketball and we started playing once a week. We did guy
things, you know. I once even went to a strip club with him and he
paid some beautiful stripper to lap dance on me. That was a complete waste of twenty bucks. Marc hated "faggots." His word, not
mine. We were at the gym once, and there was this real femmy guy

wearing a thong in the sauna and when he left, Marc said, "Ty, man, I hate faggots. Freaks of nature, man. I wish they'd just disappear." *(Long pause.)* So, I just lay there on the couch, and my mind kept floating. And I wondered what my life would have been like if I'd been honest with myself—and everyone else. And I settled on not going back to my grandmother's funeral because basically I was gay and didn't want to deal. And I started feeling guilty on so many levels, and I prayed. I don't know why. I haven't prayed in years. But I asked for a sign. Just like I did when I was a kid. Back when I went to church. When I believed. Then this feeling of peace, of serenity just swept all over my body and I opened my eyes, flipped on the TV and "The Wizard of fuckin' Oz" was on. Right at the part where Glinda was singing, "Come out, come out, wherever you are." I swear to God. So I got up and went over to the soap. It was like this quest... this, I don't know, spiritual quest. I was just—drawn. And I walked in, and people started coming up and saying, "Ty! How are you, man?!" And I just blurted out, "Fine, I'm gay!" I didn't plan it, I just did it. And it felt so good. So I went up to Marc's office, and he was so glad to see me. And I said, "Marc, I have something I have to tell you. I'm gay!" And he just laughed and said, "That's funny, that's funny shit." But I didn't laugh and he stopped and said, "You're shittin' me, aren't you? Please tell me you're shittin' me." And I shook my head. Then the weirdest thing happened. He sat there, just staring at me. Then after what seemed like sixty or seventy hours, he said, "I'm a good person, Ty. I don't know why I..." There was this long pause and I realized he couldn't talk anymore because he was all choked up. So, I said, "It's okay, man." And he said, "No, it's not! I wish I didn't have those feelings, but I do—and I'm not sure they'll ever go away. I'm sorry." Then...*(Chokes up.)* ...he said, "But I know I love you Ty...and that's not gonna go away either." Then he got up, came over, and hugged me. *(Pause.)* Then we set a racketball date. I assured him I had never had a crush on him. *(Pause.)* I lied. Then he said, "Mazel tov!" and I left.

(Lights fade to Black as an organ plays "Rock of Ages." Lights come up with the swell of the music. The stage is empty except for a few flower arrangements, a coffin downstage, between the coffin and audience a huge wreath with pink and blue carnations and a lettered ribbon—and two church pews — benches — one downstage left and one upstage right — the missing ones are an illusion, missing intentionally. TY's chair is turned backwards, downstage right, hugging the wall. The round table is now by the door with a spray of flowers and a guest book sitting on it. A wooden cross adorns the back wall. The organ music subsides as a puff of cigarette smoke proceeds SISSY, who enters dressed in black, puffing away. She looks around, signs the guest book, looks at the cross, realizes she is smoking, starts to exit—then sees no one, makes her decision and continues to smoke as she walks towards the coffin. She stares at her sister for a moment and takes a long drag.)

SISSY. Hey. Guess you don't mind if I smoke. It was just not the right time to quit...with you dyin' and all. I only lasted three days. I failed again. But after five husbands, what else is new? *(A bit emotional.)* It has not been a good day, Sister. And I'm blamin' you. I am. I cain't help it. Now you know I am not one to judge, and quite frankly, I'm glad you cut loose and had so much fun towards the end. But I just wish you'd been more careful. I mean, you turn on a light when you get up to go to the bathroom! Especially in a strange motel room. When you have affairs, you have got to be more careful. *(Another drag, mutters.)* Of course, this is useless information to you now, so why the hell am I wastin' my breath? *(Spots the wreath in front of the coffin, goes over and reads the banner.)* "Jesus Called, Peggy Answered." Awww. *(She ashes her cigarette in it, then steps back and evaluates the corpse.)* Well, for once in my life, I'm gonna have to agree with Latrelle. You look plum silly in that mink stole. *(Shudders.)* Lord. *(Studies her.)* And I don't like your lipstick.

(She digs through her bag and pulls out a tube of lipstick and a tissue and proceeds to wipe off Sister's lipstick and reapply new.)

SISSY. *(cont.)* I tell you, Walter never did have a good flair for make-up when it came to doin' bodies. I don't think he pays a bit of mind to skin-tone, much less what you're wearin'. Of course, that mink stole could throw anybody off. *(She finishes.)* There. You look real good. *(Deep breath, holding back emotion.)* I loved you, Sister, I did. I do—

(LATRELLE suddenly storms in the door.)

LATRELLE. *(Yelling.)* Sissy!

SISSY. *(Jumping.)* Good Lord, Latrelle, don't you have better sense than to yell at someone when they're talkin' to a corpse?

LATRELLE. We've got a situation, Sissy! Mama's funeral starts in thirty minutes and LaVonda's in jail!

SISSY. In jail! What on earth for?!

LATRELLE. She and Noleta Nethercott held up Tiny's Liquor Store and they're both in jail!

SISSY. Oh, Lord.

LATRELLE. So, I need you to get over there and bail her out! *(Pulls out an envelope from her purse.)* Here. Nine hundred dollars, cash. Had to go to the bank. Now go!

SISSY. Okay.

(SISSY takes the money and starts to leave.)

LATRELLE. Wait! Come back. First, I need you to help me get that stole off!

SISSY. Oh, Latrelle, LaVonda's not gonna like—

LATRELLE. I don't give a damn at this point what LaVonda likes! And you can tell her that for me too, will ya? And if she has a problem with that, then she can just rot in the pokey! Now give me a hand!

SISSY. Okay.

(LATRELLE goes around the coffin, looks at her mama for a moment.)

LATRELLE. You have caused me so much grief, Mama. You have no idea what I've had to concoct to salvage your reputation. Okay, Sissy, grab the stole on the count of three. One, two, three...

(LATRELLE lifts the corpse and SISSY reaches in and grabs the stole in one nice swoop.)

SISSY. Got it!

LATRELLE. Good, good job. Now go get La—

G.W. *(Screaming O.S.)* PEGGY!!!!!!!!

(LATRELLE and SISSY jump.)

LATRELLE. Oh, good Lord!

SISSY. Heavens! That's G.W.

LATRELLE. I don't need this! Not now, not ever. I'll handle him, go get LaVonda! And take the stole with you. Throw it in the trunk of your car. Hurry!

SISSY. I'm hurrying!

(G.W. enters, drunk. SISSY starts to exit with the stole, passing him on her way.)

SISSY. Hey, G. W. How are you?

G.W. PEGGGGGYYYYY!!!

LATRELLE. Stop that screamin', G.W., right now! Show some respect, for cryin' out loud! Now you are drunk and I want you outta here. I have no use for you. Understand?

G.W. Who the hell are you?

LATRELLE. I'm Latrelle. Peggy's oldest girl.

G.W. The tight ass.

LATRELLE. *(Indignant.)* Well!

G.W. I'm gonna burn up my legs. Gonna burn the sumbitches up 'cause they killed the woman I loved.

LATRELLE. You are not! And quit using such vulgar language in the church house.

G.W. Yes, I am. Gonna burn 'em up, just like firewood! And don't tell me I'm not! I am! Gonna douse 'em with lighter fluid and light 'em up right here in front of God and Peggy, so she can witness it and know how sorry I am.

LATRELLE. She can't witness anything' cause she's dead, G. W.!

G.W. I know she's dead, goddamn it! And it's on 'count of these sorry ass legs of mine! *(Screaming.)* PEGGGGGYYYY!!!! I am so sorry!

(LATRELLE rushes to the door to look for "help," exits for a beat. G.W. pulls a can of lighter fluid from his jacket pocket, lifts his pants leg, and starts squirting his legs. He pulls out a lighter.)

G.W. *(To PEGGY.)* I'm gonna burn 'em up for you, baby. You'll see how sorry I am. I'm gonna burn the sumbitches up. You'll see, baby.

(He starts flicking the Bic; LATRELLE re-enters, spots him and screams, then rushes over.)

LATRELLE. Stop!!! Now you give me that!

(LATRELLE grabs the lighter fluid and lighter.)

G.W. Goddamn child proof lighters.

LATRELLE. Today's been hard enough. Now git! Damnit, I mean it!

G.W. Okay, okay. I'll leave. Just let me say something' to Peggy, okay? Then I'll go. Just let me say my farewells to the only woman I ever loved.

LATRELLE. Okay, but you make it quick and I mean it!

(LATRELLE sits on the front bench and waits, still holding the lighter fluid and lighter.)

G.W. *(Pause, looks at PEGGY)* Peggy...Peggy...Peggy...Peggy, Peggy, Peggy, Peggy, Peggy. *(Pause, then turns to LATRELLE.)* I can't think of nothin' else to say.

LATRELLE. *(Gets up, ushers him down the aisle.)* It's probably for the best. Now go on, G.W. Think of your family. You need your legs. And go get Noleta out of jail.

G.W. Okay. I'm sorry I called you a tight ass.

LATRELLE. That's okay. Just go.

(G.W. starts to exit, sobbing, then turns back.)

G.W. *(Yelling.)* Life's a big of pile of shit—Latrelle!

(Then he exits.)

LATRELLE. *(Mutters.)* Well, he's right about that.

(LATRELLE signs the guest book, hides the lighter fluid and lighter behind the flowers, then looks toward the coffin.)

LATRELLE. I could just kill you—if you weren't already dead. *(Walks to the coffin.)* What got into you, Mama? Why on earth would you run around with the likes of Bitsy Mae Harling, a convict, and G.W. Nethercott, who just tried to set fire to his wooden legs in the church house to make amends for killing you. That is not a smart man, Mama! You taught us better that to cavort with trash like that. How could you leave me in a quandary like this? Huh? Do you realize what I'm gonna have to do to save your face? Huh? To save my own and that of the rest of the family. Oh, who am I kidding? I'm the only one left with any decency whatsoever. LaVonda's in jail, Brother Boy's in a mental institution. It's minutes away from your funeral, Mama, and I'm the only one who's not locked up! The only one.

(TY walks in and stands in the back watching his mother for a moment.)

LATRELLE. *(Chokes up.)* And you never gave me credit for anything.
TY. Mama.
LATRELLE. *(Turning.)* Ty!

(LATRELLE rushes over to TY.)

TY. I made it. I made it after all.
LATRELLE. *(Hugs him.)* Oh, honey. You did! Thank you. Oh, let me look at you.

(LATRELLE takes TY's face.)

TY. Are you okay?

LATRELLE. Okay? Okay?! No, Ty, I am *not,* okay. It has been a horrible, horrible day! But you're here now and things are looking up!

TY. Mama...I'm gay!

LATRELLE. *(Quick beat, then plows ahead, turns and heads for coffin.)* You don't know what I've had to deal with while your Daddy's off building houses for poor white trash with Jimmy and Rosalyn Carter. Your Aunt LaVonda held up a liquor store and is in jail. *(Re: wreath.)* Aren't these flower's pretty...

TY. Mama...are you listening? I'm gay.

LATRELLE. *(Faster.)* And I gave your Aunt Sissy the bail money—nine hundred dollars, which I better get back—and we were able to pry that god-awful mink stole off of your grandmother that your favorite Aunt LaVonda insisted...

TY. Did you hear me...?

LATRELLE. *(Overlap.)* ...she wear in the heat of summer.

(TY grabs his mother by the shoulders and looks her in the face.)

TY. Mama! I'm gay!

LATRELLE. I know you're gay, Ty!!! I've known you're gay since you were five years old and you wanted that doll Suzy Q for Christmas instead of the dump truck that your Daddy wanted to buy you! I know you're gay, Ty, I've always known, but could we just please bury your grandmother and get on with life! Huh? Could we? Because I think I'm gonna explode any minute if ANY MORE SHIT HITS THE FAN TODAY!!!

TY. You knew? Since I was five? I've had twenty-seven therapists and you knew? Did you just say "shit"?

LATRELLE. I did. And I said damn today and hell and bitch and dookey—and I gotta tell you, I feel like sayin' a whole lot more! Damn, hell, shit, bitch, dookey, damn, hell, shit, bitch, dookey, damn, hell, shit, bitch, TITTY!!!!

TY. Okay, okay, calm down. *(Pause, hugs her.)* Thank you.

LATRELLE. *(Regains composure.)* For what?!

TY. I don't know. For sewing those "Slim" labels on my "Husky" jeans.

LATRELLE. *(Smiles.)* Oh, my Lord. I forgot all about that.

TY. I didn't.

LATRELLE. Slim. Lord, Ty, you were fatter than Baby Huey. Do you think for one minute we fooled anybody?

TY. No.

(They laugh.)

LATRELLE. Oh God, it feels good to laugh.

TY. Yes, it does.

LATRELLE. I hadn't laughed all day.

(LATRELLE goes and sits on the front pew.)

TY. *(Stops laughing, pause.)* Why *did* you change those labels, Mama?

LATRELLE. *(Thinks.)* All I ever wanted for you was for you to be happy. And I couldn't make you happy. *(Chokes up.)* And I blame Dr. McCright!

(TY goes and sits by LATRELLE.)

TY. Dr. McCright. For what?

LATRELLE. For you being gay. When I was pregnant with you, he gave me this drug that had estrogen in it to keep me from miscarrying again. And I'm positive that's what caused this. I could just kill him! *(Remembers.)* If he wasn't already dead.

TY. *(Laughs.)* Mama, I don't think that's what caused *this*. And I'm getting happy now. I want you to know that.

LATRELLE. Well, I'm glad someone is.

(Awkward pause. TY turns and looks at the coffin, gets up and evaluates.)

TY. Nan Nan looks good.

LATRELLE. Now. Lord, what she did to Brother Boy. She would roll over in her grave if she knew you were gay too. That is, if she were in her grave.

(TY saunters over, smirking mischievously.)

TY. *(To corpse.)* Hey, Nan Nan. Guess what? I'm gay. Gay as a goose.

LATRELLE. *(Laughs.)* Stop that!

TY. Gay as Uncle Brother Boy!

LATRELLE. *(Rising.)* You are not! Nobody's that gay! *(Looks around, then crosses to TY hush-hush.)* So, what is it exactly that you do?

TY. What?

LATRELLE. You know, when you're gay?

TY. Oh dear God! I hope my mother isn't asking me about my sex life.

LATRELLE. If I'm gonna have a gay son, then I need to know about gay sex.

TY. Then read a book, Mama! I don't ask you what happens in the privacy of your own bedroom.

LATRELLE. I'll tell you exactly what happens — nothin'!

TY. No, no, no, no, no. I'm not about to explain gay sex and the details of my own sex life to my mama in front of my grand-mother's coffin

    LATRELLE. You wanna step outside?

    TY. No! I'm not going to discuss this with you! Period!

    LATRELLE. Okay, fine. Be that way.

(LATRELLE goes and sits on the front pew, arms crossed.)

    TY. I will!

    LATRELLE. I was just trying to be open.

    TY. Well, I don't want you to be!

(Pause. TY realizes and smiles. LATRELLE motions. He goes and sits by her on the pew. She puts her hand on his face and studies him.)

    LATRELLE. You were always my special boy. I've never felt closer to anyone. No one. We've always had that...bond. *(Chokes up.)* And you know, I'm not sure we would of had that if you weren't gay. So, I don't regret taking that drug after I lost all those other babies. Because I can't imagine life without you, Ty.

    TY. *(Emotional.)* I like who I am now, Mama. So, instead of blaming Dr. McCright, maybe we should thank him.

    LATRELLE. Maybe. But he's dead.

(TY hugs his Mother, hard.)

    TY. I love you, Mama. So much.

    LATRELLE. I love you too, baby.

(They continue to hold each other, then finally break.)

    LATRELLE. Are you the woman or the man?

(Blackout.)

(Organ music — "In the Sweet, By and By" — swells as Lights Come Up on the funeral. The PREACHER enters and stands in front of the coffin. [Note: Double cast Odell, play him old maybe, gray wig — stage where you never see Preacher's face.] LATRELLE and TY are still in the front row, LATRELLE now on TY's other side by the aisle as SISSY rushes in.)

PREACHER. *(Singing.)* "In The Sweet, By And By..."
SISSY. *(Calling out door.)* Come on, LaVonda! They've already started.
ALL. "We Shall Meet On That Beautiful Shore."

(As SISSY passes by the PREACHER, she nods and starts singing the echo ("By and By"). LA VONDA enters, same clothes as "Two Wooden Legs", only has buttoned her blouse to cover bra and cleavage. Her hair is a mess; she straightens it as she walks towards her mother.)

PREACHER. *(Nods at SISSY.)* Everybody sing, now.

(SISSY sees TY and hugs him, then sits.)

ALL. "In The Sweet, By And By..."

(LA VONDA arrives at the casket, notices the stole is missing, glares at LATRELLE. TY heads off a confrontation by going to LA VONDA and hugging her. She hugs him back, hard, then mutters something about the stole as they take their seats as the song continues.)

ALL. "We Shall Meet on That Beautiful Shore. A-men."
PREACHER. Yes, brethren, we shall meet on that beautiful shore. Praise Jesus. Praise the Lord. Today we are gathered here

together to pay our respects to and celebrate the life of our beloved
sister, Peggy Sue Ingram.

*(BITSY MAE HARLING walks in the door. Her head down, she is
crying, and carries a guitar. She signs the guest book, bumps
the table with her guitar. LATRELLE turns back and looks.)*

LATRELLE. *(Overlap.)* Who is that?!
PREACHER. *(Overlap.)* Peggy was born February 28th, 1931
right here outside of Winters.
SISSY. *(Overlap, loud whisper.)* Bitsy Mae Harling.
LATRELLE. Who?
LA VONDA. Bitsy!
LATRELLE. Oh, Lord!
PREACHER. Peggy married Theodore Edward Ingram June
30th, 1948 right here at Southside Baptist Church. Peggy is sur-
vived by her daughters, Latrelle Sue Williamson, LaVonda Jean
Dupree and a son, Earl Don "Brother Boy" Ingram, who unfortu-
nately could not be with us today.
LATRELLE. *(Heavenward, mutters.)* Praise the Lord.
PREACHER. She has one grandchild, Theodore Edward
Williamson, an actor...hi Ty.
TY. *(Embarrassed.)* Hi.
PREACHER. And a surviving sister, Marie "Sissy" Hickey.

*(SISSY raises her hand. G.W. and NOLETA enter and sit on the
back pew; NOLETA pissed at G.W.)*

PREACHER. Peggy died July 23rd, 1996. At this time,
Peggy's eldrest daughter, Latrelle, would like to say a few words
in memory of her dearly departed mother.
LATRELLE. *(Rises, walks over and stands by casket.)* Thank
you, Bro. Barnes. *(To congregation.)* And thank you all for coming

here today. What a nice turnout. *(Deep breath.)* As many of you know, my Mama was not "right" for the last six months of her life. She abandoned her sense of morality and upbringing and started hanging around riff-raff.

(NOLETA lets out a loud sob. TY is explaining to LA VONDA, who is appalled; LA VONDA whispers to SISSY.)

LATRELLE. A few months ago, I took Mama to the doctor over in Snyder and they found a lemon-sized cancerous tumor on her brain!

BITSY. No!

LATRELLE. Yes! And it was inoperable and growing rapidly. Mama asked me to tell no one and I kept her secret. 'Til now. (To *corpse.)* But it's time to clear your name, Mama! *(Back to congregation.)* And what happened was the tumor grew and pressed up against the...well...the...um, sexual...part of her brain.

SISSY. Oh, my God.

LA VONDA. This is supposed to make us look better.

LATRELLE. That tumor turned my mama into a nymphomaniac. So, I ask on behalf of my grieving family that y'all forget about the circumstances surrounding her death and remember her for the good Christian that she was before that tumor destroyed her health and her morality. Thank you.

(LATRELLE sits. TY gives her a reassuring hug. The PREACHER stands again.)

PREACHER. Thank you, Latrelle for those revelations. Cancer can be so cruel. And now, I'd like to read to you—

(PREACHER goes to get his Bible, which is resting on the edge of the coffin, and knocks it in.)

PREACHER. Oops. *(Reaches in and gets it, straightens some-thing.)* From the first chapter of the Gospel of John—

BITSY. May I say a few words too, Reverend?

(PREACHER looks to the "family". LATRELLE shakes her head "no"; LA VONDA "yes".)

PREACHER. I suppose so. Yes.

(BITSY carries the guitar to the coffin.)

LATRELLE. What's she doin' now?

LA VONDA. She's gonna say a few words, too.

LATRELLE. Well, this isn't open mike!

BITSY. *(To family.)* I had no idea about the tumor. I am so sorry. But I gotta tell you, Peggy touched my life. The nympho-maniac Peggy, with all due respect. We were close. *(Poignant.)* Very close. *(The family exchange questioning looks. Could it be? BITSY continues with a fond memory.)* After we used to close up at Bubba's, I was all wound up after a big show...and well Peggy, me...sometimes G.W. over there...hi G.W.

G.W. *(Embarrassed.)* Hello, Bitsy.

(NOLETA just glares at him.)

BITSY. We'd all just sit around, get drunk and sing hymns.

SISSY. Lord, lord, lord.

BITSY. This was Peggy's favorite hymn, and I'd like to sing it as she enters those Pearly Gates to meet her maker.

(BITSY strums the guitar, startling the PREACHER, who has fallen asleep.)

BITSY. "Just As I Am". Listen to the words. They apply on so many levels.

LATRELLE. *(Mutters.)* I'm gonna wake up any minute now.

BITSY. "Just As I Am, Without One Plea, But That Thy Blood, Was Shed For Me, And That Thou Bidd'st Me Come To Thee, O Lamb Of God, I Come! I Come!"

(BROTHER BOY walks in the door, escorted by WARDELL. He is wearing a black señorita dress, with the blonde wig perfectly coiffed, red flower in the wig. He stops, listens to the song, whispers something to WARDELL, who then goes and stands behind G. W. and NOLETA. Everyone turns around to look.)

LATRELLE. *(Whispers, panicked overlap.)* Is that... !?

LA VONDA. *(To TY.)* That is your Uncle Brother Boy!

(LATRELLE flies up and rushes him.)

LATRELLE. *(Screams.)* NOOOOOO!!!!! Get him outta here! Get him outta here!!! He's a spectacle!

BROTHER BOY. *(Overlap.)* Don't you start, Latrelle!

(All hell breaks loose with screaming and yelling. SISSY grabs LATRELLE's arm and turns her around.)

SISSY. Latrelle, stop it! Just stop it right now or I'm gonna knock you into next week!

LATRELLE. But...

SISSY. Shut up, sit down and let 'im stay!

TY. He's family, Mama. Let him stay. *(Meaning it.)* Mama, let him stay!

(LATRELLE stops, suddenly calms, looks at TY then at BROTHER BOY.)

LATRELLE. *(Softly.)* Okay.
BITSY. *(Mutters.)* Tough crowd.

(There is an awkward silence as everyone takes their seats. The PREACHER nods at BITSY who starts singing again. One by one, everyone joins in softly, letting the emotion and their grief take over. First LA VONDA, then SISSY, then TY then G.W., NOLETA and WARDELL.)

BITSY. "Just As I Am, Tho' Tossed About, With Many A Conflict, Many A Doubt, Fightings Within And Fears Without, O Lamb Of God, I Come! I Come!

(BROTHER BOY walks towards the coffin, trying to get a peak at his mother. He tiptoes, then proceeds some more. He arrives in front of her, and sadly looks at her, joining in singing on "I come, I come." He takes out a tissue from his purse, starts to bend down towards her, then stops and sneers as the Lights Go Down, leaving him in a Spotlight.)

BROTHER BOY. Well, I guess you didn't think I was gonna make it, did ya, Mama!?

(He wheels around and starts to exit.)

(Blackout.)

END OF PLAY

APPENDIX-A

JUANITA VERSION

After the success of the movie "Sordid Lives," I had so many requests from various productions to include the character of "Juanita" (so deliciously portrayed in the film by Sarah Hunley) that I decided to give theatres the option to include the character by adding her to Chapters Two and Four in this new publication.

I suggest that Juanita wear a short jean skirt with a peach t-shirt that has been shredded and beaded on the sleeves and at the bottom. Her hair should be very high — and she believes, as I do, that eye shadow does not have to stop at the brows.

Del Shores

CHAPTER TWO

Two Wooden Legs

(A guitar strums in the darkness. A spotlight hits BITSY MAE who is standing in the theatre aisle, leaning against the wall. [Note: While BITSY sings, onstage the cast and crew strike the set and set up the next one].)

BITSY. *(Slow and sad.)*
"O they tell me of a home far beyond the skies,
O they tell me of a home far away;
O they tell me of a home where no storm-clouds rise,
O they tell me of an uncloudy day.
O the land of cloudless day,
O the land of an uncloudy day;
O they tell me of a home where no storm-clouds rise,
O they tell me of an uncloudy day.

O they tell me that He smiles on His children there,
And His smile drives their sorrow all away;
And they tell me that no tears ever come again,
In that lovely land of uncloudy day.

O the land of cloudless day,
O the land of an uncloudy day;
O they tell me of a home where no storm-clouds rise,
O they tell me of an uncloudy day.

(Key change, dramatic and soulful)

O the land of cloudless day,
O the land of an uncloudy day;
O they tell me of a home where no storm-clouds rise,
O they tell me of an uncloudy day."

(The spotlight fades. BITSY exits. Lights come up on TY, sitting in his chair downstage center talking to his therapist again.)

TY. When I was a kid, I was fat. A fat boy. Waddlebutt. That's what the other kids called me. I wish they could see my ass today. I've worked really hard on my ass. *(Realizes.)* Anyway. One year — I think I was in fifth grade — my Mama took me shopping for school clothes and I had gotten fatter and I had to try on jeans and the only ones that would fit were the "Husky" ones. And they had this label on the back that said, "Husky!" Kinda announced to everyone behind you that you were a "Husky!" And I started crying. Because I didn't want the other kids to know I was a "Husky." So, my Mama sat me down right there in the store, hugged me and told me that no one ever had to know. Just me and her. Our little secret. And she bought me those "Husky" jeans, took them home. Went to the Goodwill and bought some used jeans, took the labels off the "Husky" ones and she sewed on "Slim" labels from the Goodwill ones. "Slim." Shit. Like I could pull that off. *(Laughs, then mood change.)* But that's the kind of mama she was. She never made me feel bad about being fat. Always made it okay. And I've always thought that was unconditional love and maybe if I told her I was gay it'd, you know, apply. But there's this other thought that keeps running through my head — that she'd try and change the labels. You know, instead of from "Husky" to "Slim", from gay to straight, so no one would know. I mean, I tried to do that for years.

(Lights dim to Blackout as a country song plays loudly. LIGHTS come up to reveal G.W. NETHERCOTT, late 40's, rugged, a man's man, standing in despair by the jukebox in Bubba's Beer Joint. Ty's chair is moved and is sitting at a round bar table, downstage center, where ODELL OWENS, 40's, performs string tricks like Jacob's ladder, cat's cradle, cup 'n saucer etc. singing along to the song. His brother, WARDELL "BUBBA" OWENS, late 40's, the proprietor here, wipes down the bar, also singing. There are two bar stools in front of the bar, one is occupied by JUANITA BARTLETT, this bar's fly, always drunk, 50, 60? Hard to tell. The song ends, G.W. crosses to the table.)

ODELL. That'sa good un'.
WARDELL. Real good.
G.W. Not since Nam. No, sir. Not since Nam. Shit.

(He joins ODELL at the table as JUANITA takes her beer, crosses over to the jukebox and studies the song selection.)

JUANITA. I wonder whatever happened to ol' Lynn Anderson?

(WARDELL crosses, handing G.W. a fresh beer.)

WARDELL. I don't know, Juanita. Here ya go, G.W.

(WARDELL pats G.W. on the back.)

G.W. I just can't get'er offa my mind, Wardell.
WARDELL. Well, that's some serious-ass shit you been through, boy.

G.W. I'm in agony.

WARDELL. I can tell.

G.W. I'm in hell. I remember it so vividly. We met at the Bonanza over in Abilene, had us a nice steak supper, then she followed me back to the motel and...

JUANITA. Lynn Anderson had such pretty blonde hair. Just like golden silk.

ODELL. *(Showing his latest string accomplishment.)* Jacob's ladder. *(Takes a piece of string with his mouth and pulls.)* Witch's hat. You do Jacob's ladder, then witch's hat. Two tricks in one. Well, one trick. Then another by just pullin' the string with ya teeth. Ain't that neat.

G.W. You have too much time on your hands, Odell.

(JUANITA has wandered over, stands behind ODELL and evaluates the string.)

JUANITA. Idn't that somethin'.

ODELL. *(Starts another trick.)* You know what I can't get offa my mind?

WARDELL. Oh boy, here we go again.

ODELL. I can't get that pig bloatin' incident offa my mind.

G.W. What?

WARDELL. G.W., please. If I have to hear about that goddamn pig one more time, I think I'll just shit!

ODELL. It all happened over at the Tyler County Fair.

WARDELL. Well, now's just as good a time as any. *(He grabs a newspaper from the bar and exits to the bathroom.)* Y'all keep an eye on the place.

ODELL. Sure thang, Bubba.

JUANITA. *(Leans over: to G.W.)* Was your steak tender? The one you ate that night Peggy died?

(G.W. just looks at her, shakes his head.)

ODELL. See, I go down to Tyler ever' year for the County Fair. *(Showing another string trick.)* Broom. I just love all the animals and the displays of macrame and the cookin' competition and all. 'Sides it gives me a chance to see me and Wardell's sister.

JUANITA. I onced made a rooster outta beans and lentils when I was a girl. At Vacation Bible School. It was almost life-like.

G.W. I see. *(Back to ODELL.)* How is ol' Mozelle?

ODELL. Oh, she's fine.

G.W. You know, me and Mozelle — we had us some good times once upon a time.

ODELL. You know her and Darrel have had a buncha marital problems. He beat her up a few times, but after me and Wardell went over there and showed him what a good ass-whoopin' was all about, he's been a perfect husband and father ever since. You know how Bubba feels about his little sister. *(Showing another string trick.)* Teepee.

JUANITA. Mama hung ol' Cockadoodle up in the kitchen — that's what I called 'im — Cockadoodle — but the bowl weevils started eatin' them beans...*(Gets emotional.)*...and that was all she wrote.

G.W. *(A glance to JUANITA.)* Amazing. *(Back to ODELL.)* Well, I never thought that Darrel Koontz never was worth a good goddamn anyhow. Any man who beats a woman is no man at all.

ODELL. He's in group therapy for abusive husbands now. A buncha wife beaters gets together once a week with this specialist in wife beatin' and they purge. Some of 'em are dead-beat dads too. There used to be two groups, one for wife beaters and one for dead-beat dads, but so many crossed over from one group to the next, that they merged. *(Thinks.)* Hey, they merged and they purged.

G.W. Purged?

ODELL. Uh-huh. That's when you all kinda spew forth your story and then you feel better after'n you spew forth. Darrel says it works. Hadn't laid a hand on Mozelle since he started purgin'. Said it disgusts him now. 'Course I think that whoopin' mighta had somethin' to do with it.

JUANITA. I've seen bowl weevils in flour...and oatmeal... and paprika, but never on a rooster you made in Vacation Bible School.

G.W. Well, I probably shoulda married Mozelle instead of Noleta, then maybe I wouldn't been compelled to fool around and Peggy woulda still been alive. Life is a big ol' pile of shit, Odell.

ODELL. You know, G.W., no offense, but you're startin' to get on my nerves. I mean, get off the cross, buddy — we need the wood! *(Pause.)* That was a joke, G.W. You know, to lift your spirits.

(G.W. just glares at him as JUANITA and ODELL laugh.)

G.W. Uh-huh. Well you of all people have a lot of gall to say that I'm gettin' on your nerves when you stay on ever'body's nerves about 99.9 percent of the goddamn time!

JUANITA. *(Claps her hands.)* Boys, boys.

ODELL. I'll have you know, a lotta people find me to be a very interesting person.

G.W. Who?

ODELL. Vera Lisso over at the Piggly Wiggly.

G.W. Bullshit.

ODELL. Why when I told her my pig story, she was absolutely riveted!

G.W. That's 'cause she can't get up!!

ODELL. *(Turns away.)* You've done gone and hurt my feelings now. *(He pouts.)*

JUANITA. *(Pats ODELL on the back.)* My mama sure hurt my feelings when she threw out ol' Cockadoodle.

G.W. Okay, Odell, I'm sorry. Go ahead, tell me your pig story.

ODELL. Nuh-uh. Ain't gonna tell it.

G.W. Oh, come on.

ODELL. I'm gonna save it for someone who really wants to hear it.

G.W. Just tell it. Don't be a baby.

ODELL. Nope. Ain't gonna do it.

G.W. Alright, fine, suit yourself. I don't give a shit.

ODELL. *(Pause.)* It all happened at the swine weigh-in.

(JUANITA crosses to the bar, goes behind it, helps herself to a fresh beer, listens.)

G.W. The swine weigh-in?

ODELL. You know where they weigh the hogs to make sure they qualify for the competition. They have to meet these Future Farmer's of America guidelines, you know.

G.W. Ah ha.

ODELL. Well, this one kid was told that his pig was a few pounds light and wouldn't get to compete unless it gained a few pounds right quick like.

G.W. Uh-huh.

ODELL. *(Finishes another string trick.)* Cup-in-saucer. Pocketbook. Two tricks in one. Didn't even use my teeth. Ain't that neat.

G.W. *(Angrily grabs the string, wads it up and throws it on the floor.)* What happened to the pig, Odell?

JUANITA. The other white meat.

ODELL. I'm gettin' to that, G.W. *(He takes another string out of his pocket.)* Well, as I rounded the corner to where they was all lined up for the porta potty, that's when I witnessed the whole shebang.

JUANITA. And I strongly believe that Mama just didn't like ol' Cockadoodle and made up that bowl weevil shit 'cause I sure the hell never saw no goddamn bugs!

G.W. I'm in hell.

(JUANITA rounds the bar, sits on one of the stools, takes out her compact, checks her make-up.)

ODELL. And that kid and a bunch of his buddies. They all looked like juvenile delinquents to me. They was holding that pig down while they was sticking a garden hose and pushin' water down that poor ol' pig's throat. Well, I yelled out, "Hey what you boys doin' to that pig?" And the biggest one said, "Don't you never mind. This here's my pig. Just go drain ya pipe." Told me to go drain my pipe. Well, about that time — *(Chokes up again.)* I'm sorry, but the vision — it haunts me, G.W.

WARDELL. *(Re-enters.)* You mean to tell me, you ain't finished?

(JUANITA fishes for a tube of lipstick in her purse, pulls it out, and while never taking her cigarette out of her mouth, masterfully moves it from one side to the other as she re-applies.)

ODELL. I got sidetracked.

WARDELL. Naw!

ODELL. Shut up, Wardell.

WARDELL. Don't you tell me to shut up or I'll whoop your ass!

ODELL. Go to hell, Wardell!

WARDELL. Lead the way!

JUANITA. Hey! Do y'all thank I'm perty?

ODELL. *(Back to G.W.)* So, I started to go on my way and just forget about the whole thang when that poor ol' pig fell over, started wallerin' around and convulsin', then...*(Close to tears.)*...it just lay down and...and —

WARDELL. Died. The damn pig died! Kaput! Done! Finished! End of story. Next!

ODELL. Didn't even get to compete in the fair.

WARDELL. Yeah, well that's a damn shame. But I guess now that life can go on, huh, G.W.?

G.W. Except for the pig's. *(Starts laughing.)*

WARDELL. *(Joins in.)* Except for the pig's.

JUANITA. *(Joins in.)* That's a good 'un. Shit!

ODELL. Well, it ain't funny!

WARDELL. Oh, yeah it is. That's the first time G.W.'s laughed since Peggy died.

(G.W. suddenly stops laughing and begins to cry.)

G.W. Shit...shit...

ODELL. *(Pats G.W. on the shoulder.)* It's okay, buddy. I know how you feel, G. W. I still have nightmares over that pig myself with water spewin' out of it's nose and snout —

G.W. *(Exploding.)* I don't give a shit about that filthy, dirty, slop-eating, mud-wallerin' pig, Odell! I have killed a woman by irresponsibly leaving these legs in the middle of the motel room after we made long passionate love.

WARDELL. Oh my Lord.

G.W. And I haven't killed a person since Nam. And I didn't love any of them slant-eyed gooks. And killin' them has haunted me for years. So how am I s'pose to go on after killin' someone I love? Huh? You'll get over that pig, Odell. I ain't ever gonna get over killin' Peggy.

WARDELL. G.W., go easy on yourself, buddy. She tripped on your legs on her way to the bathroom. It's not your fault. It was an accident. Coulda happened to anyone.

ODELL. Anyone with two wooden legs, you mean.

WARDELL. Shut up, Odell.

ODELL. Go to hell, Wardell.

WARDELL. Lead the way!!!

JUANITA. *(Suddenly angry.)* Mama was a goddamn liar!

WARDELL. *(Irritated.)* Juanita, you're gonna have to let that go.

ODELL. I'll tell you another thing I can't get offa my mind —

WARDELL. Oh, shit.

ODELL. That Ebola virus...

WARDELL. I swear to Christ, if you go into that one again, I'll beat you half to death.

ODELL. It all started in Zaire —

(NOLETA and LA VONDA storm in. They are both drunk and NOLETA brandishes a pistol, while LA VONDA is waving a shotgun. They have obviously given each other make-overs and wear sunglasses.)

NOLETA. Put your hands over your heads and don't make any sudden moves!

LA VONDA. *(Overlap.)* Now! Move it!

WARDELL. Shit..!

(ODELL quickly throws his hands over his head, G.W. and WARDELL just stare at the women for a moment. JUANITA is unfazed.)

G.W. What the hell do you think you're doin', woman?

NOLETA. We just watched "Thelma and Louise" and we're pissed.

LA VONDA. At men.

NOLETA. All men! Especially the three of y'all. Hey, Juanita.

JUANITA. Hey shug, how ya doin'?

ODELL. Why are you pissed at me? What did I ever do?

NOLETA. You live and breath, Odell, so just shut up and quit askin' questions. We'll ask the questions, okay?!

ODELL. Okay.

NOLETA. You make me sick, G.W. Just looking at ya makes me wanna kill ya dead!

G.W. C'mon. Noleta —

NOLETA. It's Thelma!

LA VONDA. I thought I was Thelma.

NOLETA. No, Thelma's the one with the shitty husband. Hey, I said hands up, G.W.! You too, Wardell. Now!!! I mean it.

WARDELL. Okay, okay.

LA VONDA. Why, hello, Wardell.

WARDELL. Hey, LaVonda. You're lookin' good.

LA VONDA. Yeah, well, I work at it. So, you and your nit-wit brother over there beat up any queers lately?

ODELL. Hey! I ain't no nit-wit.

LA VONDA. LIAR!!!

G.W. Y'all are drunk.

NOLETA. No shit. And I'm on Valium too. You have no idea how much I hate your stinkin' guts right now G.W.

G.W. Noleta, come on, we can talk about this —

NOLETA. *(Smacks him up side the head.)* Shut up!

G.W. Ow!

WARDELL. LaVonda. you know I've always felt real bad

over that incident with Brother Boy.

LA VONDA. You feel bad, huh? He feels bad.

JUANITA. Bad.

LA VONDA. You feel bad and he's rottin' in a crazy farm because of you! Big deal, Wardell! It's time to get even!

WARDELL. But that happened over twenty years ago.

LA VONDA. I don't want to hear it, Wardell, so just shut the hell the up! *(She pumps the shotgun.)* And I mean it!

WARDELL. Okay, okay, just don't shoot.

ODELL. I don't like this.

G.W. *(Laughs, to WARDELL.)* I don't know why you're over there peein' in your Wranglers. Them guns ain't loaded and even if they was, they wouldn't have the gumption to shoot.

NOLETA. Wanna bet!? *(She shoots across the room and some bull horns fall from the wall.)* Whooeee! In the words of Thelma, I thank I've got a knack for this shit.

LA VONDA. You sure do. Nice shot, Thelma.

NOLETA. Thanks, Louise, but I was aimin' for his head.

(JUANITA goes over and kicks the bull horns.)

JUANITA. There goes the neighborhood.

G.W. Noleta, now come on —

NOLETA. It's THELMA, you shithead!!!

G.W. Okay, okay, Thelma, then. Look, I know I messed up, but you gotta know that I wasn't exactly gettin' what a man needs at home.

NOLETA. What?!!

LA VONDA. Uh-oh.

JUANITA. Ouch.

NOLETA. I hope you ain't gonna try and justify your actions, G.W.,'cause buddy boy, you ain't got a leg to stand on.

LA VONDA. Except them wooden ones.
JUANITA. Oh, that's a good'un.

(They both laugh.)

NOLETA. Except them wooden ones. That is funny. *(Laughs.)*
G.W. Goddamn! This is worse than Nam.
NOLETA. Hey, Wardell! Get me a shooter! 'Cause I'm startin'
to get happy here and we cain't let that happen.
WARDELL. God forbid. *(Pours shooter.)*
LA VONDA. Get me one too, Wardell.
JUANITA. While you're at it, Wardell —

(WARDELL pours two more.)

G.W. For God's sake, woman, c'mon —
NOLETA. Shut up! Until I say otherwise! 'Cause I have
somethin I gotta say.

*(She crosses to bar, she and LA VONDA clink glasses, then down
shooters. JUANITA wanders over and downs hers.)*

NOLETA. *(To WARDELL.)* Thank you.
JUANITA. That hit the spot.
NOLETA. *(Back to G.W.)* Why'd you do it? *(G.W. starts to say
something.)* Don't answer that! Just think about it. Do you know
what it means to be humiliated, G. W.? Don't answer that! Just
think about it. Well, I do. I can't even go out in my own hometown
now because everyone knows. Everybody pointin' and whisperin'.
"There she is." "Poor pitiful thang." "Bless her heart." God! White
trash even feel sorry for me!
JUANITA. That's true. That is very very true.

NOLETA. Everyone knows that you were carrying on with my best friend's mother. That coulda ruined me and LaVonda's friendship, you know. Did you think of that? Don't answer that! Just think about it. But it didn't. And you wanna know why? Because we're big enough not to let it.

G.W. *(Mumbles.)* You got that right.

LA VONDA. Oooh — he shouldn'ta said that.

JUANITA. No, ma'am. He should have not.

NOLETA. What'd you say?!

G.W. I said y'all're certainly big enough. Why do you think I did it, huh? You got as big as a barn and who the hell wants to climb that mountain?

NOLETA. That's it! Take off your shirt!

G.W. What?

NOLETA. I said, take off your shirt!! NOW!!! *(She puts the pistol right to G.W.'s head.)*

G.W. Jesus! Okay, okay. *(He gets up and starts taking off his shirt.)*

JUANITA. This is gettin' good.

LA VONDA. *(Waving the shotgun at ODELL and WARDELL.)* You too, boys. Take off ya shirts.

WARDELL. *(Starts to take his off.)* What're y'all doin'?

LA VONDA. Getting even! Odell!? What the hell you waitin' for? Christmas?!

ODELL. Okay, okay. *(He starts taking off his shirt.)*

G.W. This is ridiculous.

NOLETA. Ridiculous? I'll tell you what's ridiculous. It's ridiculous for you to bitch about my weight when you look like you're six months pregnant. *(She pokes his stomach with the pistol.)* Look at that gut, LaVonda.

LA VONDA. *(Evaluates.)* Lord! It's time to butcher that hog!

JUANITA. Suckin' in too.

NOLETA. I raised your kids, G. W. I stayed as faithful as the day was long. Cooked ya supper ever' night. And you just shit all over our weddin' vows. Just shit all over'em. *(To LA VONDA.)* I tried to lose weight. I went to Jenny Craig's and lost twenty-two pounds. *(Smacks and screams at ODELL.)* Twenty-two goddamn pounds! And he never even noticed. Never said one word.

G.W. Yeah, well, that'd be kinda like the Titanic losin' a coupla deck chairs.

LA VONDA. You really are a shit, G.W. I wonder what my Mama saw in your sorry ass, anyway?

NOLETA. Off with your pants, G.W.

G.W. Wha...I ain't gonna—

NOLETA. TAKE OFF YOUR GODDAMN PANTS, ASS-HOLE!!!

(She fires the gun. A piece of ceiling comes crashing down.
JUANITA laughs.)

JUANITA. I'd take'em off if I was you.

G.W. *(Taking them off.)* Jesus...God...damn...shit...!!

LA VONDA. You too, boys. Quit ya grinnin' and drop ya linen.

WARDELL. Oh, man. What did I do to deserve this?

LA VONDA. You ruined my brother's life, Wardell. Along with your nitwit brother there. So, take 'em off!!!

(The brothers start taking off their pants.)

ODELL. I don't much appreciate you callin' me a nitwit.

JUANITA. How about half-wit?

ODELL. I don't like that either.

G.W. *(Throws pants on the floor.)* There! Are ya satisfied?

NOLETA. You ain't satisfied me in years.

LA VONDA. I loved you, Wardell, but you had to ruin it all by beating the shit outta Brother Boy.

WARDELL. I beat the shit outta him because you said he was in love with me.

LA VONDA. You know what Mama said the day the sheriff brought Brother Boy home all beat to a bloody pulp? *(Waving gun at ODELL.)* Huh? Do you?!

ODELL. *(Scared shitless.)* No, I don't!

LA VONDA. She said, "Well, that just proves my point. He just can't live in regular society like a normal human bein'. It's too dangerous." *(Emotional.)* And the very next day, her and Daddy drove him over to Big Springs and signed the papers for him to rot in that crazy farm. *(Drops emotion, intense anger.)* And I will never forgive you for that, Wardell! And I'll never forgive myself for tellin' you he was in love with you. You ruined his life, Wardell!

WARDELL. You think I don't think about that ever' day of my life? Huh? I thought the world and all of Brother Boy. Loved him like my very own brother. Hell, more than this idiot. *(Indicates ODELL.)*

ODELL. You loved that queer more than me?

WARDELL. Brother Boy was my first friend. My best friend. And when he turned queer, it liked to killed me. I just felt so betrayed. But I never meant to hurt him, Vonie. I just lost it when you told me that. I flipped out.

ODELL. I flipped out too!

WARDELL. I'm sorry, LaVonda. But can I please get dressed? I mean, what if someone walked in? This is a place of business for cryin' out loud.

(He starts to put on his pants. LA VONDA snatches them with the shotgun barrel and flings them across the bar.)

LA VONDA. Tough titty!

JUANITA. Said the kitty.

NOLETA. Hey Louise, you wanna take the pictures or hold the gun?

G.W. Pictures?

LAVONDA. I guess I'll hold the gun. *(Stares at WARDELL'S crotch.)* Since mine's bigger.

NOLETA. Okay.

(She starts digging around in her purse, pulls out a black lacy bra and throws it at G.W.)

NOLETA. Here, titty man. Put this on.

G.W. *(Catching it.)* What?! I ain't puttin' on...You can't be serious —

(NOLETA fires her pistol in the air.)

G.W. Damn...

WARDELL. *(Overlap.)* Shit...

ODELL. *(Overlap.)* Ahhhh!!!

JUANITA. She seems perty serious to me.

WARDELL. Just put on the brassiere, G.W.!

G.W. Fine. Fine! *(Glaring at NOLETA as he puts it on.)* You are one mean-ass bitch!

NOLETA. You're just lucky I ain't Latin and got a butcher knife.

G.W. *(Struggling with hooking bra.)* Shit...

LA VONDA. Help 'im with the hooks, Wardell. I know you

know how to do that. At least you know how to undo 'em. (*Cattle prodding him with shotgun over to G.W.*) Quit pussy footin' around! Now c'mon! Hook'em!

WARDELL. (*Hooking up G. W.*) Okay, okay...shit!

JUANITA. Good fit.

ODELL. (*Laughing.*) You oughta see yourself, G.W. Damn... (*Laughs more.*) Thank God I don't have a mean-ass bitch wife too.

JUANITA. These boys just don't learn.

NOLETA. (*Turning.*) What did you say?

ODELL. I take it back!

NOLETA. Too late! Sit your ass down.

(*She pushes him in a chair, then starts digging through her bag and pulls out some earrings and a turban and hands them to LA VONDA, then pulls out a handful of makeup.*)

NOLETA. (*To LA VONDA, indicating WARDELL.*) These are for him.

(*She hands her pistol to LA VONDA, so she can make-over ODELL.*)

ODELL. Please! LaVonda, I'm sorry about that Brother Boy incident. Wardell made me —

LA VONDA. Hush up, Pauline Pitiful.

NOLETA. (*To ODELL.*) Pucker up.

(*He does. She smears lipstick on his lips.*)

LA VONDA. (*Hands earrings to WARDELL.*) Here, put these on.

WARDELL. This ain't right, LaVonda.

NOLETA. *(To ODELL.)* Okay, go like this. *(She presses her lips together, then smacks, ODELL complies.)* Nice. That's Misty Rose from Avon. Just in case you like it, you'll know.

JUANITA. Good color on him.

NOLETA. *(As she paints ODELL'S eyebrows, laughing, mumbles.)* Pauline Pitiful. *(To LA VONDA.)* That's funny.

LA VONDA. *(Evaluating WARDELL'S earrings.)* What'daya think, Thelma?

NOLETA. Oh yeah, nice. Turban.

JUANITA. *(Laughs.)* You girls crack me up.

LA VONDA. *(Hands the turban to WARDELL.)* Put this on. *(Spots G.W.'s wooden legs across the bar, crosses, stalking him.)* So, those are the culprits that killed my Mama. *(She bangs the legs with the shotgun.)*

G.W. Hey, I'm a veteran, goddamnit!

LA VONDA. *(Re: turban.)* Oh, turn that around, Wardell. The jewel goes in front.

WARDELL. Oh. *(He complies.)*

JUANITA. Much, much better.

(NOLETA finishes ODELL by clipping a poofy red flower in his hair. She turns the severely painted face towards LA VONDA.)

NOLETA. What'daya, think, Louise?

LA VONDA. *(Evaluates.)* That is one ugly bitch!

NOLETA. Okay. Odell, go sit over there. *(Points to a bar stool.)* Wardell come on outta there and sit on this bar stool. *(WARDELL complies.)* It's time for a group picture.

(She pulls out a Polaroid camera from her bag.)

G.W. I'm beggin' you, baby.

NOLETA. Save it for someone who gives a shit! Now get on over there with your boyfriends and give 'em a group hug. Come on! Now! Before I make ya do somethin' even more humiliatin'. I'm starting to get pissed again!

(G.W. takes his place between the brothers. NOLETA snaps a picture, pulls it out and hands it to JUANITA, who starts shaking it.)

LA VONDA. *(Waving the gun.)* Y'all can do better than that! Put ya arms around each other. Act like you love one another. *(They comply.)*

NOLETA. *(Snapping another picture, hands it to JUANITA.)* Now, G.W., look in Wardell's eyes longingly like you did with that tramp you cheated on me with.

LA VONDA. Hey, that was my mama!

NOLETA. Sorry. Do it, G. W.! *(He makes a feeble attempt, she snaps a picture and hands it to JUANITA.)* Now say, "I love you, Wardell!"

G.W. Ain't no way —

(LA VONDA fires the pistol.)

G.W. *(Quickly.)* I love you, Wardell!

NOLETA. That's more like it.

JUANITA. *(Staring at the pictures "developing".)* Oh, these are looking good.

LA VONDA. They sure are.

G.W. Shit. Are we done yet?

NOLETA. Almost. Just as soon as you reach over and kiss Odell. On the mouth!

G.W. Okay, that's it!

(He crosses to LA VONDA, grabs the gun and sticks it to his head, LA VONDA still holding it.)

G.W. Go ahead. Shoot me! Just kill me dead right here and now 'cause I'll be goddamn if I'm gonna kiss Odell!

WARDELL. *(Losing it.)* Oh, shut up, G.W...and take your punishment like a man!

G.W. Like a man? Like a man? Well, that's a little hard to do, Wardell — WHILE WEARING A BLACK BRASSIERE!!!

JUANITA. That makes so much sense.

WARDELL. Yeah, well, you made your bed, so just by-gawd lay in it! And maybe she's doin' you a favor. Did you think about that? Huh?!

G.W. A favor?! What the hell are you talkin' about? A favor.

WARDELL. All I'm saying is that at least she's getting even right after it happened. I beat the shit outta my homo best friend and sent him packing to the loony bin for the rest of his life. And I have been livin' with that guilt for twenty some odd years now! *(To LA VONDA.)* I wish you had done this sooner. Then maybe my life woulda been better than this. *(Back to G.W.)* So, maybe your life's gonna be better, G.W., by wearing that perty little lacy black brassiere. That's all I'm sayin'. What can I do, LaVonda? What can I do to make it better? What can I do for you? What can I do for Brother Boy? *(Emotional.)* Maybe I can do somethin', LaVonda. Just tell me what I can do.

LA VONDA. *(Softly.)* Ain't nothin' you can do, Wardell. Not now.

(She pats him on the back with the pistol.)

WARDELL. I am so sorry.

LA VONDA. I just wish Brother Boy knew.

WARDELL. Me too.

LA VONDA. *(Composing herself.)* Well, I think we've done some good here today. I feel like I been to church.

JUANITA. *(Hands to heaven.)* Amen! Praise Jesus!

NOLETA. *(To JUANITA.)* Lemme have my pictures. *(JUANITA hands them over; to LA VONDA.)* You feed the jukebox. Time for a little dancin'.

G.W. Dancin?

NOLETA. *(Re: pictures.)* These are good.

JUANITA. *(Looking over NOLETA's shoulder.)* You boys are real photogenic.

ODELL. What you gonna do with them pictures, Thelma?

NOLETA. Sell 'em, asshole, what the hell do you think?!

ODELL. What are you gonna do with all our stuff, Louise?

LA VONDA. Burn it, Pauline! *(Re:jukebox)* Oh, here's a good 'un.

(LA VONDA makes her selection and the music begins.)

NOLETA. G.W., you and Odell — dance. And then we'll be gone.

(G.W. approaches ODELL, they stare at each other.)

G.W. Damn, shit, hell, fire! *(Pause)* I'll be the man.

ODELL. Lookin' like that?

(G.W. grabs ODELL, and starts clumsily dancing with him.)

NOLETA. *(A little emotional.)* He never took me dancin'. Not once. And that hurts.

LA VONDA. Men! Okay, Wardell, ask Odell if you can cut in.

Go ahead on. It'll ease that guilt.
>WARDELL. Then I'll gladly do it. *(Goes over.)* Odell —
>ODELL. Yeah?
>WARDELL. Can I cut in?
>ODELL. *(Quickly.)* Sure thang, Wardell.

(He rushes away and sits on stool.)

>G.W. Shit...

(WARDELL and G.W. start dancing.)

>LA VONDA. I had to do it, Wardell. For Brother Boy.
>WARDELL. I'm glad you did. I feel better now.
>G.W. Jesus H. Christ!

*(The girls put on their sunglasses, NOLETA puts her arm around
LA VONDA and turns the camera towards them.)*

>NOLETA. Hey, Louise.
>LA VONDA. Yeah, Thelma.

(She take the classic "Thelma & Louise" picture.)

>NOLETA. Let's go on over to Tiny's Liquor and stick him up.
He shortchanged me the other day.
>LA VONDA. Why that son-of-a-bitch. Let's go!
>JUANITA. I'll drive the get away car. Y'all are drunk!

*(JUANITA grabs her purse and the girls all exit as lights start to
dim, leaving WARDELL and G.W. only in a spotlight as the
music continues. WARDELL and G.W. continue to dance a
couple of moments, then WARDELL lays his head on G.W.'s
shoulder.)*

WARDELL. I shoulda never beat up Brother Boy.

(Blackout.)

END OF CHAPTER TWO

CHAPTER FOUR

All Laid Out (In a Mink Stole)

*(AUTHOR'S NOTE: Chapter Four remains the same until
    JUANITA'S entrance.)*

LATRELLE. *(Rises. walks over and stands by casket.)* Thank
you, Bro. Barnes. *(To congregation.)* And thank you all for coming
here today. What a nice turnout. *(Deep breath.)* As many of you
know, my Mama was not "right" for the last six months of her life.
She abandoned her sense of morality and upbringing and started
hanging around riff-raff.

(JUANITA enters, still in the same outfit when she left the bar.)

LATRELLE. A few months ago, I took Mama to the doctor
over in Snyder and they found a lemon-sized cancerous tumor on
her brain!
JUANITA. No!
LATRELLE. Yes! And it was inoperable and growing rapidly.
JUANITA. *(Whispers to G.W.)* Scooch over, shug.

(He does and she sits by him, gives a little wave to NOLETA.)

LATRELLE. Mama asked me to tell no one and I kept her
secret. 'Til now. *(To corpse.)* But it's time to clear your name,
Mama! *(Back to congregation.)* And what happened was the tumor
grew and pressed up against the...well...the...um, sexual...part of
her brain.
SISSY. Oh, my God.

LAVONDA. This is supposed to make us look better.

LATRELLE. That tumor turned my mama into a nymphomaniac. So, I ask on behalf of my grieving family that y'all forget about the circumstances surrounding her death and remember her for the good Christian that she was before that tumor destroyed her health and her morality. Thank you.

(She sits. TY gives her a reassuring hug. The PREACHER stands again. JUANITA pops a beer that is in her purse and begins to discreetly take sips during the rest of the funeral.)

PREACHER. Thank you, Latrelle for those revelations. Cancer can be so cruel. And now, I like to read to you —

(He goes to get his Bible, which is resting on the edge of the coffin, and knocks it in.)

PREACHER. Oops. *(Reaches in and gets it, straightens something.)* From the first chapter of the Gospel of John —

BITSY. May I say a few words too, Reverend?

(PREACHER looks to the "family". LATRELLE shakes her head "no"; LA VONDA "yes".)

PREACHER. I suppose so. Yes.

(BITSY carries the guitar to the coffin.)

LATRELLE. What's she doin' now?

LA VONDA. She's gonna say a few words, too.

LATRELLE. Well, this isn't open mike!

BITSY. *(To family.)* I had no idea about the tumor. I am so sorry. But I gotta tell you, Peggy touched my life. The nymphoma-niac Peggy, with all due respect. We were close. *(Poignant.)* Very close.

(The family exchange questioning looks. Could it be?)

BITSY. *(Fond memory.)* After we used to close up at Bubba's, I was all wound up after a big show...and well Peggy, me... Juanita...sometimes G.W. over there...hi G.W.

G.W. *(Embarrassed.)* Hello, Bitsy.

(NOLETA just glares at him.)

BITSY. We'd all just sit around, get drunk and sing hymns.
SISSY. Lord, lord, lord.
JUANITA. Those were the good ol' days.
BITSY. This was Peggy's favorite hymn, and I'd like to sing it as she enters those Pearly Gates to meet her maker.

(She strums the guitar, startling the PREACHER, who has fallen asleep.)

BITSY. "Just As I Am". Listen to the words. They apply on so many levels.
LATRELLE. *(Mutters.)* I'm gonna wake up any minute now.
BITSY. "Just As I Am, Without One Plea, But That Thy Blood, Was Shed For Me, And That Thou Bidd'st Me Come To Thee, O Lamb Of God, I Come! I Come!"

(BROTHER BOY walks in the door, escorted by WARDELL. He is wearing a black señorita dress, with the blonde wig perfectly coiffed, red flower in the wig. He stops, listens to the song,

whispers something to WARDELL, who then goes and stands behind G.W., NOLETA and JUANITA. Everyone turns around to look.)

LATRELLE. *(Whispers, panicked overlap.)* Is that...!?
LA VONDA. *(To TY.)* That is your Uncle Brother Boy!

(LATRELLE flies up and rushes him.)

LATRELLE. *(Screams.)* NOOOOO!!!!! Get him outta here! Get him outta here!!! He's a spectacle!
BROTHER BOY. *(Overlap.)* Don't you start, Latrelle!

(All hell breaks loose with screaming and yelling. SISSY grabs LATRELLE's arm and turns her around.)

SISSY. Latrelle, stop it! Just stop it right now or I'm gonna knock you into next week!
LATRELLE. But...
SISSY. Shut up, sit down and let 'im stay!
TY. He's family, Mama. Let him stay. *(Meaning it.)* Mama, let him stay!

(LATRELLE stops, suddenly calms, looks at TY, then at BROTHER BOY.)

LATRELLE. *(Softly.)* Okay.
BITSY. *(Mutters.)* Tough crowd.

(There is an awkward silence as everyone takes their seats. The PREACHER nods at BITSY, who starts singing again. JUANITA lifts her hands in praise. One by one, everyone joins in softly, letting the emotion and their grief take over. First

LA VONDA, then SISSY, then TY, then G.W., NOLETA, WARDELL and JUANITA.)

BITSY. "Just As I Am, Tho' Tossed About, With Many A Conflict, Many A Doubt, Fightings Within And Fears Without, O Lamb of God, I Come! I Come!"

(BROTHER BOY walks towards the coffin, trying to get a peek of his mother. He tiptoes, then proceeds some more. He arrives in front of her, and sadly looks at her, joining in singing on "I come, I come." He takes out a tissue from his purse, starts to bend down towards her, then stops and sneers as the Lights Go Down, leaving him in a Spotlight.)

BROTHER BOY. Well, I guess you didn't think I was gonna make it, did ya, Mama!?

(He wheels around and starts to exit! Blackout.)

END OF PLAY

APPENDIX-B

The following is alternative dialogue suggested by the author for more "conservative"productions. Also, Mr. Shores grants permission for any other "language" to be deleted or replaced (example "goddamn" could become simply "damn") as long as the changes do not alter the story, characters or the integrity of the play.

CHAPTER ONE—Nicotine Fit

P.9

Ty's Line: "In fact, the first time I heard the word "fuck", it came out of her mouth."

Alternate: "In fact, the first time I heard the "F" word, it came out of her mouth."

Ty's Line: "And the most beautiful cock you have ever seen. Ruth was hung like a horse."

Alternate: "And the most beautiful, well, you know, you have ever seen. Ruth was certainly blessed."

Ty's Line: "He was all flabby and pasty, and he had this little bitty thumb dick."

Alternate: "He was all flabby and pasty, and well, Artie was not blessed. At all."

Ty's Line: "I woke up with a hard-on, totally turned on by Ruth Buzzi's old prude woman as a man."

Alternate: "I woke up totally turned on by Ruth Buzzi's old prude woman as a man."

CHAPTER THREE —The Dehomosexualization of Brother Boy

P. 56:

Line: "And I looked at him and realized that I had fucked up. "

Alternate: "And I looked at him and realized that I had screwed (messed) up."

P. 57

Line: "Why the fuck do I care?"

Alternate: "Why the hell do I care?"

P. 67

Eve's Line: "I want you to fuck me, Earl. Because quite frankly, I think it's time you fuck a woman."

Alternate: "I want you to do me, Earl. Because quite frankly, I think it's time you do a woman."

Eve's Line: "Now let's go! FUCK ME!!!!"

Alternate: "Now let's go! Let's do it!!!!"

P. 68

Eve's Line: "Fuck me, Earl! Fuck me NOW!!!!"

Alternate: "Do me, Earl! Do me NOW!!!!"

Eve's Line: "I know. Now just take yours off and fuck me, Earl!!! FUCK ME!!!"

Alternate: "I know. Now just take yours off and let's do it right now!!!!"

CHAPTER FOUR—All Laid Out (In a Mink Stole)

P. 77

Ty's Line: "... and "The Wizard of fuckin' Oz" was on."

Alternate: "... and "The Wizard of Oz" was on."

COSTUME PLOT

BITSY MAE
Nicotine Fit
Black suede micro mini
Black fishnets
Yellow & black two-tone cowboy boots
Black leather bra
Tattoo

Two Wooden Legs
Same
Lose leather bra
Add Black & yellow shell
Add gold vest

The Dehomosexualization of Brother Boy
Same

All Laid Out (In a Mink Stole) - Funeral
Same
Lose gold vest & shell
Add Black shear long sleeve blouse

TY
Nicotine Fit
Faded Levi 501 jeans, button fly
White long sleeve collared shirt (untucked)
Old brown work boots
Silver ring (left hand)

Two Wooden Legs
Same

The Dehomosexualization of Brother Boy
Same

All Laid Out (In a Mink Stole) - Monologue
Faded Levi 501 jeans, button fly
Tight muscle black T-shirt
Silver ring
Black socks
Black shoes

All Laid Out (In a Mink Stole) - Funeral Scene
Black double-breasted suit
Same black T-shirt
Same black shoes
Same black socks
No ring

SISSY

Nicotine Fit
Khaki Culottes
Sleeveless cotton green palm tree print blouse
Pink oversized glasses
Rubber band (left arm)
Wedding ring (left hand)
Pearl ring (right hand)
Dangly coral earrings
Khaki canvas sandles

All Laid Out (In a Mink Stole)
Black polyester dress with ruffled collar and sleeves
Black patent low heels
Gold hoop earrings
Wedding ring
Pearl Ring
Black purse (inside: tissue, lipstick, Altoid Case for putting
    out cigarette, lighter)

LATRELLE
Nicotine Fit
Light pastel flowered jacket
Light blue skirt
Navy belt
Beige blouse with half embroidered collar
Pretty half slip
Beige purse
Beige low heels
Watch
Engagement ring and wedding band set
Gold necklace
White pretty handkerchief

All Laid Out (In a Mink Stole)
Summer black short-sleeve suit
Black blouse
Black belt
Black pumps
Same handkerchief
Same jewelry

LA VONDA
Nicotine Fit
Canary yellow ruffled sleeveless peasant-style blouse
Tight Lee jeans
Flashy belt
Gold & white sandals w/2" heel
Large gold earrings
Gold chain w/gold Texas charm
Several rings
Watch
Purse—cigarette case & lighter inside

Two Wooden Legs
Black lace Western blouse—unbuttoned about 3 buttons
    and folded back to reveal:
Red lacy teddy with Wonderbra
Tight black jeans
Large rhinestone dangly earrings
Red hair ornament
Black boots "Thelma & Louise" black sunglasses encrusted
    with rhinestones (matching Noleta's)
Rings, Texas chain and watch from Nicotine Fit

All Laid Out (In a Mink Stole)
Same as Two Wooden Legs (blouse is buttoned)
Lose earrings, hair ornament and sunglasses

NOLETA
Nicotine Fit
Cut-off tight blue faded jeans

Sleeveless faded pink print blouse
Bright blue sheer hair bonnet
Pink curlers
Old white keds with no laces
Kleenex inside bra

Two Wooden Legs
Hot pink skirt and blouse with silver & turquoise Western
    trim
Silver belt
Hot pink cowboy boots
Big earrings
Bracelet
Necklace with Western motif
Hot pink hair clip
False eyelashes
"Thelma & Louise" sunglasses (matching LaVonda's)

All Laid Out (In a Mink Stole)
Same as Two Wooden Legs
Lose earrings, bracelet, necklace, hair clip, eyelashes and
    sunglasses

WARDELL
Two Wooden Legs
Beige cowboy shirt
Wrangler jeans
Cowboy belt with big buckle
Jockey shorts
Old time pattern socks
Brown cowboy boots

The Dehomosexualization of Brother Boy
Same
Add straw cowboy hat

All Laid Out (In a Mink Stole)
Same
No hat

ODELL

Two Wooden Legs
Powder blue polyester pants with elastic waist
Light yellow short-sleeve shirt, with tiny brown stripes
Teal boxers
White socks
Brown cowboy boots

G. W.

Two Wooden Legs
Short sleeve 4-pocket, light green pleated guayabarra shirt
Dark brown Western-style polyester dress slacks
Western leather belt
Cotton colored print boxers
Black military Oxfords
Legs—Laminated molded polyester, slides completely over
   feet; split in back with velcro closures, leather fly strips
   (The VA hospital made for LA production)

All Laid Out (In a Mink Stole)
Tan polyester suit
White dress shirt
Same Western leather belt

Loud silk tie
Pocket handkerchief that matches tie
Same Oxford shoes

JUANITA
Two Wooden Legs
Short jean skirt
Peach t-shirt, shredded & beaded on sleeves & bottom
Cheap heels
Long dangly earrings
Cross necklace
Several rings
Bracelet
Cheap watch
Beige purse (inside: lipstick, cigarettes, lighter, beer for
     Chapter 4)

DR. EVE
The Dehomosexualization of Brother Boy
Navy blue two-piece suit (Short fitted peplum style jacket,
     short wrap skirt)
Navy pumps
Lacy red push-up bra
Lacy red garter belt
Lacy red thong panties (optional)
Navy thigh-high stockings
Silver button earrings
Silver watch
Silver ring
Purple/blue/red scarf (inside jacket covering neckline)

BROTHER BOY

The Dehomosexualization of Brother Boy

Light pink housecoat trimmed in fuschia marabou feathers

Light green cheap polyester lounging pajamas

High-heeled cork wedgies trimmed with same fuchsia
marabou feathers as housecoat

White frilly socks

Wig cap made from cut-up knee-high nylon hose, tied in top
knot

Cheap gray vinyl purse (inside: lipstick, mirror, perfume
spray, fingernail file, rat tail comb, Aqua Net Hair
Spray- red can)

Wighead with poofy Tammy Wynette blonde wig (carries),
half fixed with a few pins and sponge curlers (to be taken
out during scene)

All Laid Out (In a Mink Stole)

Black ruffled shiny señorita polyester dress (off the shoulder,
slit to thigh)

Black fishnet stockings

Black strapless brassiere stuffed with socks

Red high heels

Black purse filled with Kleenex

Big blonde wig very styled and poofy (Note: LA production
used two identical, this one the finished product, the other
so Brother Boy could finish fixing in therapy session)

PREACHER

All Laid Out (In a Mink Stole)

Dark gray suit

Light gray shirt

Red and gray print tie
Black socks
Black dress shoes
Half reading glasses
Gray wig

PROPERTY PLOT

Chapter One — Nicotine Fit

ONSTAGE

Couch
    afghan
    2 throw pillows
Coffee table
    assorted magazines
    plate (crumpled napkin 1/2 eaten biscuit—Sissy clears
        to kitchen offstage)
    glass of tea (1/2 full with ice cubes)
    hand-held church fan
Chair (Ty uses for monologue—reset onstage as part of
    living room during blackout)
Self-standing ashtray (next to couch)
Kitchen table
    set of 8 small serving plates
    apple pie (cut into slices)
    pie server
    6 forks
    napkin holder (with napkins)
    plate of fried chicken
    mashed potatoes
    bowl of biscuits
    several covered bowls and dishes
    tablecloth #1 (flowered print)
2 kitchen chairs
Small table
    phone
    box of Kleenex with crocheted cover

pictures
Sissy's purse (bottle of valium pre-set inside)
ashtray
Jesus picture upstage center

OFFSTAGE
Bitsy's guitar
Sissy's kitchen
 3 glasses of iced tea (Noleta, Sissy, LaVonda)
Small suitcase (Latrelle)
Travel Bag (Latrelle)
Latrelle's purse (pre-set with envelope of "money" for
 Chapter 4)
LaVonda's purse
 cigarettes
 lighter

Chapter Two — Two Wooden Legs

ONSTAGE
Table (same as chapter one w/o cloth)
 1 Lone Star Beer (almost empty)
2 wooden chairs (1 used by Ty for monologue—reset by
 table during blackout)
Bull horns upstage center (rigged to fall on first gunshot)
Bar
 On top of bar
  bowl of pretzels
  tequila liquor bottle
  ashtray
 Underneath the bar

4 capped Lone Star Beers
  magazine (Wardell takes to bathroom)
2 shot glasses (3 for "Juanita" version)
  bar towels
2 bar stools
Jukebox
Neon Budweiser sign
Trap door above stage with loose plaster (rigged to fall for
  second gunshot)

OFFSTAGE

Fake legs (G. W.—LA production's were made by V.A.
  Hospital to fit over actor's legs and feet)
Shotgun (LaVonda—can be replica)
Pistol (Noleta—loaded with blanks)
Noleta's bag
  Polaroid camera loaded with film
  earrings (for Wardell)
  turban (for Wardell)
  makeup kit (lipstick, eyebrow pencil, blush, large makeup
    brush)
  black lacy brassiere (for G. W.)
  earrings (for Odell)
  poofy hair flower (for Odell)

Chapter Three —
The Dehomosexualization of Brother Boy

ONSTAGE

Couch
  afghan #2

4 throw pillows
Dr. Eve's chair (used by TY for monologue—re-set by couch
    during blackout)
Coffee table
    ashtray
Dr. Eve's table "desk"—same as other scenes with:
    tablecloth #2 (preset funeral tablecloth #3 underneath)
    box of Kleenex
    egg timer
    calendar
    phone/intercom
    compact mirror
    bottled water
Dr. Eve's purse
    flask (preset inside purse)
    pill bottle (preset inside purse)
Naked lady picture upstage center

OFFSTAGE
Brother Boy's wig
Dr. Eve's notes
Dr. Eve's mini tape recorder
Pistol (Wardell)

Chapter Four—All Laid Out (In a Mink Stole)

ONSTAGE
Sign-in table — same as other scenes with:
    tablecloth #3 (tablecloth #2 removed during blackout)
    guestbook
    pen
    flowers

2 church pews (Note: LA production used benches, no backs)
Preacher's chair (used by Ty for monologue, reset during
    blackout)
Wooden cross upstage center

OFFSTAGE
    Casket (placed onstage during blackout after Ty's monologue)
    mink stole
    Big flower arrangement (on floor in front of casket)
        ribbon on flowers that reads, "Jesus Called, Peggy
Wooden cross upstage center

Set Designs by Newell Alexander

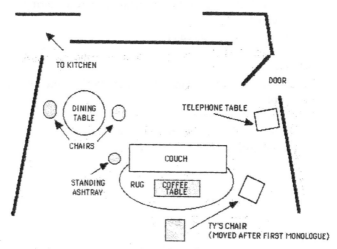

NICOTINE FIT

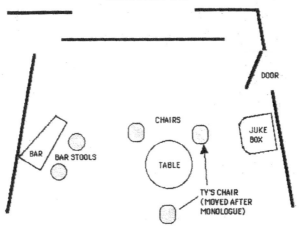

BUBBA'S BAR

Set Designs by Newell Alexander

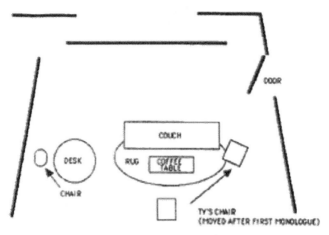

DR. EVE'S OFFICE

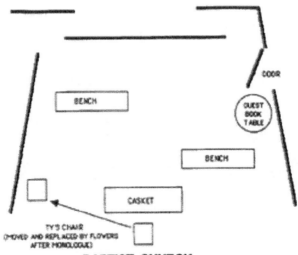

BAPTIST CHURCH

SORDID LIVES

Margot Rose / Beverly Nero
inspired by the play "Sordid Lives" by Del Shores

© 1996 Margot Rose / Beverly Nero

SORDID LIVES

SORDID LIVES

SORDID LIVES REPRISE

SORDID LIVES

SORDID LIVES
In The Sweet By And By

Just As I Am

SORDID LIVES
Lord, I'm Coming Home

Del Shores has written six plays set in his native Texas -- "Cheatin'", "Daddy's Dyin' (Who's Got The Will?)", "Daughters of the Lone Star State", "Sordid Lives", "Southern Baptist Sissies" and "The Trials and Tribulations of a Trailer Trash Housewife". His plays have been performed worldwide and have garnered Mr. Shores multiple theatre awards and nominations for his writing and directing, including the Ovation, NAACP, L.A. Weekly, Backstage West Garland, GLAAD, Robby, Drama-Logue and the Los Angeles Drama Critics Circle Awards. His movie adaptation of his play "Daddy's Dyin'" was released in 1990 by MGM. In 2000, the movie adaptation of his play "Sordid Lives" was released by Regent Entertainment and has become a cult phenomenon. Mr. Shores wrote and directed the film. He has also written and produced for many television shows, including "Ned and Stacey", "Dharma and Greg" and "Queer As Folk". Mr. Shores resides in Los Angeles with his husband Jason Dottley and his daughters Rebecca and Caroline. He may be contacted at his web address, www.DelShores.net.

Photo by: Rosemary Alexander

OTHER POPULAR TITLES BY

Del Shores

Daddy's Dyin' (Who's Got the Will)

Cheatin'

Daughters of the Lone Star State

Southern Baptist Sissies

DADDY'S DYIN' (WHO'S GOT THE WILL)
Del Shores

Comedy / 3m, 5f / Interior

"Set in a small Texas town in anytime, U.S.A., Daddy's Dyin' concerns the reunion of a family gathered to await the imminent death of their patriarch, who has recently suffered a physically as well as mentally disabling stroke. In essence, however, it is not the story of the impending demise of the father or of the drafting of his will, but of a rebirth of the spirit of the family unit. Without becoming ponderous, losing a sense of humor or pandering to timeworn cliches about Texans or Texas drawls, the story shares many elements of a good summer novel: it's a fast, delicious, easy read with funny moments, tense moments, touching moments, and characters you care about."-The Hollywood Reporter

"A masterful comedy."
- *Variety*

"A well written piece of mainstream theatre that's consistently funny and occasionally touching."
- *The Los Angeles Times*

"A knockout."
- *L.A. Weekly*

SOUTHERN BAPTIST SISSIES
Del Shores

Comedy / 7m, 2f / Unit Set

Follows the journey of four gay boys in the Baptist Church. Storyteller Mark Lee Fuller tries to create a world of love and acceptance in the church and clubs of Dallas, Texas, while desperately trying to find a place to put his own pain and rage. The world Mark creates also includes two older barflies, Peanut and Odette, whose banter takes the audience from hysterical laughter to tragedy and tears. With a theme of religion clashing with sexuality, the play opened to rave reviews in Los Angeles during its original run in 2000 and became the most awarded play of the year, winning the GLAAD Media Award for Outstanding LA Theater Production, as well as multiple LA Weekly Theater Awards, Los Angeles Critics Awards, Ovation Awards, Backstage West Garland Awards and Robby Awards.

"Daring. Heroic. No-holds-barred hilarious."
- LA Times

"Cathartic, comedic, awe-inspiring."
- Daily Variety

"Brash, sensitive and compelling. An evening of engrossing and, at times, hilarious theatre."
- The Hollywood Reporter